MAMA DIDN'T Sign Up FOR THIS

SIOBHAN SMILE

MAMA DIDN'T SIGN UP FOR THIS

SIOBHAN SMILE

HOSTILE WHISPERS PRESS, LLC

To my readers who believe everyone is worthy of love, respect, and an unconditional happily every after.

MAMA DIDN'T SIGN UP FOR THIS

He had one rule. Sometimes rules were meant to be broken.

Drake

My life changed on the first day of school. Could this be a midlife crisis? No, that was too easy an explanation. I never crossed the line of dating a mother of one of the students in my school. That was a complication I didn't need. My brain told me I needed to keep my distance, but every time I ran into Sari Hampton, every part of me screamed she was mine. There was no way I was going to be able to resist the pretty single mom.

Sari

I may write romance for a living, but I was just faking it. At thirty-nine, I was not having any success in finding my happily ever after. There was one thing in life I could control—I wanted a family. I'd grown up in foster care. And after years of fostering children like me, I'd given them a place to be safe no matter how briefly they came to me. That was until Reggie arrived, and I knew he was my son. Yet, the first day at his new school, I met Principal Drake Pike. He was too perfect. We weren't going to be friends, but how long could I remain strong and keep a safe distance between him and my heart?

SARI

T his wasn't how I'd planned the start of my day with my son's grubby hands holding my face and yelling at me, but what we planned doesn't always happen. It was his first day of school in our new town. I'd worried about him, there were too many changes in two short years, and the adoption papers were signed only a few weeks prior.

I was a freelance writer and novelist who worked from home. I rarely left the comfort of my office, but when Reggie informed me that morning that I'd needed to take him to school, I'd instantly panicked. He held onto his calm better than me.

"Focus, Mama, focus."

"We're fine, I'm fine, we're fine, right?"

"Mama, it's meeting my teacher, and then you can go home. Why are you like this?" The six-year-old sounded far older than his years, but they'd shuffled him around foster homes since birth. Something in me had melted the minute he called me Mama with complete certainty. And every roadblock in my life had led me to being his mother—we'd held our breath until the judge said he was mine.

I'd promised myself I'd make sure he had a childhood, unlike mine where I'd stayed a ward of the state until I'd graduated high school. I'd always wanted to be a parent for as long as I could remember. Being a bisexual, Black, Transgender woman, I hadn't thought it possible it would happen. They'd warned me about the hoops I'd need to jump through. How far above reproach I needed to be to adopt one day.

With my height and build, I never thought I'd pass enough to earn the acceptance of society, but I'd long ago given up the notion I needed to be anything other than myself. I'd accomplished nearly everything I'd wanted to in life, and the last thing had been to become a mom. It took years of studying and home visits; my first foster and then my tenth, and then Reggie had moved in, and I knew in my heart he was mine. While I'd loved all the children who'd come to me on their journey, with Reggie there had been a connection—a soulmate. A child shouldn't have the hope fade from their eyes the longer they experienced rejection. Even decades later, I still suffered the pain and humiliation of unwantedness.

"Be nice to me." He rolled his beautiful chocolate-colored eyes and ran his fingers through his dark blond hair as he had a habit of doing when I frustrated him.

"For a hippie, you're too much."

"You don't even know what a hippie is." I straightened, and he turned to lean his shoulder against my thigh. I raised my hands to fluff my puffs that I'd put my hair in that morning. Smoothed my tunic blouse and the bright, mirrored skirt. I couldn't remember the last time I'd done anything with myself, but mini sleep shorts, a ratty t-shirt and fuzzy slippers, and my bonnet weren't impression-making for my son's teachers.

My little blond, fair-skinned son was already going to be the odd one out with his tall, plus-sized, dark-skinned mama. His hand slipped into mine, and I glanced down to find him smiling at me. No matter what he'd gone through, he still had the ability to smile, and I'd make sure it stayed that way.

Other parents and kids entered the front doors. I'd already picked up his schedule and learned where his classroom was, so it was a matter of dealing with the crowd. We made our way across the parking lot and through the doors. His little fingers tightened on mine; he played a good game, but I knew he was as nervous as I was. Over the summer, we'd moved out of my apartment and into a house. Reggie had left all the friends he'd made in kindergarten behind, and it had to be overwhelming.

After a few nerve-induced wrong turns, we finally made it to the open door of his classroom.

"This will be good for both of us, I promise." He gave me a sharp, confident nod, and we walked through without him ever releasing my hand. I froze just inside the room at the beast of a man who blocked the way. His shoulders appeared twice as broad as me, and he had an expression on his face that made me want to back up. He was wearing an expensive business suit but looked as if he should be wearing a gladiator outfit instead.

"A new student. Hello, I'm your teacher, Miss Mabe." A pretty, petite woman about my age stepped in front of us.

"Hello, Ms. Mabe, this is my mom, Sari, and I'm Reggie Hampton."

I'd expected the look and the shock on her face, and it amused me more than it irritated me.

"Sari and Reggie, pleasure to meet you both. First days are normally scary. Parents are allowed to stay for a bit if they want at the back of the classroom."

"Mama."

I looked down as he called my name, and I crouched next to him. Once again, his chubby hands grabbed my cheeks. "Yes, love."

"You are not staying."

I let out an offended gasp. "Are you embarrassed by your old hippie mother? What if I kiss your cheeks really, really, really loudly before—" He squeezed my cheeks to cut me off.

"Mama, take a breath."

"You're good on your own." He rolled his eyes. "Fix your face, boy."

"Ha, ha, ha, you tried that already, and what happened?"

I couldn't stop my own eye roll. "You walked around with your eyes crossed for two days."

A loud snort caught my attention, and I tipped my head back to find the behemoth watching us; he didn't pretend he wasn't staring. I didn't know how I felt about his attention. Normally, I kept my head high and dared anyone to say anything to me. Yet with me crouched down, it made him seem larger and more overwhelming.

I turned my focus back to my son. "I know you're good. I'll be in the pickup lane to get you when school's over, or did you want to take the bus?"

"Pick me up. You owe me ice cream for making you coffee this morning. You need to get better at mornings. I'm a kid who requires breakfast and someone to make sure I brush my hair and teeth."

"Hopefully not with the same brush."

"Get out," he demanded. But as I started to stand, he wrapped his arms around my neck. "Thanks, Mama," he whispered in my ear, and as I pulled away, I saw just a hint of worry in his eyes.

I took his beautiful face in my hands. "You'll do great, make a bunch of new friends, and it'll feel like home in no time. Because if not, no matter what..." I paused.

"We're each other's home."

"That's right."

He rushed off with his backpack bouncing, and I straightened to watch him for a few more minutes.

"He'll be fine, Mrs..."

I cut her off to correct her. "Ms. Hampton, but please call me Sari."

"Like I said, he'll be fine. First days at a new school are always a little scary. Today will be an easy day, mostly just getting to know each other and all that."

"My son may not want to share."

"Which is perfectly acceptable. Sari, this is our principal, Drake Pike. He likes to check in on all the classrooms on the first day of school. More parents are arriving. Your son is in good hands, I promise."

The giant was the principal? I waited until she was gone and turned toward the man. Even at my height and size, I felt small beside him—which was highly unusual for me. "Mr. Pike, nice to meet you."

"I'm sure it's not. You nearly ran when you saw me." As he called me out, his voice contained a guttural edge, which fit the size of him perfectly.

"Rude of you to point out."

"Truth is not rude. It's how you take that truth and your reaction to it. Like that adorable, snarled nose. If you'll excuse me, I need to check the other classrooms. I'm sure your son will fit in nicely around here, Ms. Hampton."

I was never one to lack a comeback or something to say, so when he left before I could even react, I was pissed at myself. I stared at his back and the door he disappeared through, and I shook myself. I glanced one more time to find Reggie talking to a little Black girl who had the seat next to him.

As much as I wanted to take a spot at the back of the classroom, I respected Reggie's comfort zone, and he wanted to do this on his own. I left, making my way back through the hallways. Curiosity had me peeking into other rooms, and I stumbled as I spotted Mr. Pike. His face completely transformed with a wide smile that softened the scowl I'd earned. He was talking to a petite woman with her arm around a little girl who was a miniature version of her.

Asshole. I forced my feet to get to moving. I had a deadline to meet, then errands to run, and we still had boxes waiting to be unpacked. Also, we needed groceries. I had so much to do before picking Reggie up. I didn't have time to analyze why a stranger didn't appear to like me. I had better things to do with my time.

I had a deadline to keep, and asshole principals weren't on my list of things to worry about that day. The farther I got away from Reggie's classroom, the more I wanted to go back. He wanted to stand on his own two feet, and I showed him respect—I didn't care if he was a kid or not. In foster care, his time was always running out before the next foster home or school. He needed stability and a happy life, so I'd promised him he'd always be safe with me.

2

DRAKE

I stood at the pickup lane as students filled the buses and others got into their parents' cars. First days were always hectic, and after twenty years of teaching and the five years as principal, exhaustion still wore me down at the end. I waved and smiled or more like forced the friendly expression on my face. As I sensed I wasn't alone, glancing down, I found Reggie staring at a phone with a screen bigger than his face and earbuds in.

"Hello, Reggie. Waiting on your mom?"

He jerked his gaze up to me and nodded. "Yes. She's at the grocery store."

He flashed me the screen, and Sari's face filled the display; her bright smile fell as soon as she looked at me. I tried not to grimace. She'd accused me of being rude, and I had to admit I was. I hated when people made me conscious of my size. This town and school were all I'd known; everyone had known me my entire life, and I'd forget I was oversized. An almost fifty-year-old man shouldn't still have lingering insecurities, but I did.

I was six-five and two hundred and seventy pounds, working out four times a week hadn't stopped the rounding of my belly, and as a lineman in younger years, I'd always had a bit of a curve.

Most of the time, I hadn't paid attention to my body other than the fact it helped me attend college. I was the oldest son of three boys and two girls, and I'd told my parents to save my college fund for my siblings. Yet when my playing days ended, I was still that big guy who looked a little scary.

"No, Mama, we still have cookies." His annoyed voice brought me out of my thoughts.

I nearly barked out a loud laugh at the horror on her face. It appeared Reggie ran the house. A part of their conversation I'd overheard that morning still played in my head. The way they'd stared into each other's eyes.

"Because if not, no matter what..." she'd paused and waited for him to answer.

"We're each other's home."

He'd responded without a second of hesitation. He was a child who knew she loved and completely accepted him. I'd never had that connection with anyone, I was a life-long bachelor or serial monogamist, no children, and while my family was close, they all had partners and families. I was only months away from my fiftieth birthday, and my parents had stopped asking years ago if I'd met anyone. I saw the disappointment in my mother's eyes every year which passed where I remained single. I couldn't even remember the last time I'd had a date. Probably not since my last relationship ended two years prior. I knew she didn't want me alone.

"We didn't have food at home," the little boy said with an eye roll, and the shocked look on his mother's face showed what she thought of his statement, but I couldn't make out what she was saying. "She said she wasn't starving me, and we had plenty of food."

I chuckled as he rolled his eyes again at her glare. "Tell her I'll sit with you until she gets here," I said, as I noticed it looked as if she was getting in line before the video called ended. Unlike some kids, he put his phone away.

"She got busy. She's on deadline."

"Oh, what does your mom do?"

"She writes books. They all have naked people on the covers."

I coughed to cover my laugh at the obvious disgust in his voice. He was an incredibly intelligent child, and his teacher said he was well ahead of the other students already when she'd caught me during lunch. I'd checked his file, and his reading and math skills were at least two grades ahead. There wasn't much in his file other than he attended kindergarten in the city before transferring there.

City schools were always overcrowded and underfunded, so I wondered if that's why they'd moved there. I had no business speculating on what her reasons for relocating were. I had a strict rule about not dating students' mothers, and I wouldn't break that for anything. No matter how tempting I might have found Sari Hampton.

"How was your first day?"

"It was good."

"Make any friends?"

"A few."

"Not a man of many words, huh?" He opened his mouth to say something, then snapped it shut as if he were about to reveal something he shouldn't. He shrugged his shoulders. I didn't point it out—just watched as the parking lot, bus, and pickup lanes emptied out. When the last car disappeared, I let all the tension of the day ease away, stretching my shoulders and neck.

"You don't have to wait. Mama will be here soon."

"I don't mind. Gives me an excuse to ignore the papers on my desk."

"You sound like Mama."

"Why don't we sit over there?" I asked as I motioned toward a bench. There was another shrug, and then he was making his way to take a seat. He crawled up onto the bench, and I lowered beside him. I let him stay silent as I leaned forward and rested my forearms on my knees.

The store wasn't that far away, so I expected Sari would arrive shortly. She was unmarried, and there was no one else in his file approved to pick him up, so I didn't mind waiting with him to help. If he didn't want to talk, I wouldn't make him. He kicked his feet back and forth.

An SUV pulled up to the curb, and we stood at the same time as she walked around the front of the vehicle. In a moment of weakness, I took in the tall, thick woman with small breasts. She still had her hair in the adorable puffs from that morning. Her skirt and shirt were covered in a long purple sweater that hung to her knees. I reminded myself of my rule, but I was helpless not to check her out a bit.

"Ms. Hampton."

"Mr. Pike. Coffee and cookies as a thank you for staying with him. Gluten and nut-free in case you have allergies. I'll need to work more on my time management." I took the large to-go cup and the paper bag.

"You're welcome. As I told him, I'm avoiding the paperwork on my desk."

His sigh told me what he thought about me procrastinating, and he was walking toward the SUV.

"I'll have to work on his manners. He's, well, he's very routine-oriented. Things have to be..." she paused as if she was searching for a way to explain.

"Just so, it makes him feel safe and comfortable," I finished for her.

"Yes, that. I better go before he sees the cookies in the backseat."

I chuckled as she shrugged, and we exchanged goodbyes. When I should've walked back inside, I stood there to take in the sway of her hips as she left. I didn't know what it was about the dark-skinned woman I couldn't ignore. I was going to need to get my unexpected attraction under control. Shoving my right hand into my pocket, I turned as I saw her glance at me as she rounded the front.

I loved her height—her thickness. I wouldn't have to bend in half for a hug or kiss. I growled. In all the years I'd been a teacher and principal, I'd never experienced attraction to a parent before. Yes, I'd noticed if one of the ladies was attractive in general appeal, but I never had the urge to date or touch one of them.

I walked the halls, checking in with the teachers about their days. Afterward, I'd finish my paperwork. Then I'd head home and make dinner for one or order delivery. Cooking for one didn't appeal to me. I was happy with my life. I was content, but the loneliness was just getting to me. I was tired and needed sleep, I'd get that, and I'd be back to normal.

3

SARI

I ran into the school in a panic. Since I'd received the call from the office, my heart had been in my throat. All they'd told me was there'd been an incident between my son and two other students. I'd thought everything would be okay. A few weeks had passed without issues, then a sudden call to the principal's office.

"I'm Reggie Hampton's mother."

"Yes, they're waiting for you in Mr. Pike's office."

She pointed me in the direction of a closed door, and I approached it, took a deep breath, and entered. The scene before me froze me in my steps. There were two men with two boys standing in front of them, and Reggie sat with his shoulders slumped. I ignored everyone and rushed to him, crouched down, and placed my fingers under his chin.

He had a smear of red under his tiny pug nose. "Are you okay?" I searched him for bruises and didn't care about the people in the room staring at me. I hadn't missed the disgust in their eyes when I'd entered the room. Learning to read a room quickly had saved my life on more than one occasion.

"I've had worse."

"Reggie Harvey Hampton, that's not what I asked." He'd

learned toxic habits in a former home, and it was a work in progress to get him to admit if he'd hurt himself.

"Yes, Mama, I'm fine."

"Okay, now tell me the truth."

"They were making fun of me."

Voices started to speak behind me. "Shut up. I'm speaking to my son." The room went silent. "And why were they making fun of you?"

"They said my real parents didn't want me and that you weren't my real mom, a man..."

"Honey, say it." I'd always believed that if you named the thing that hurt you, it no longer had power over you. My hard-earned pride in everything I was wasn't something I'd hide; selfish or not, I'd hated myself too long to be shamed by close-minded people.

"They said a man couldn't be a mama."

"Am I a man, Reggie?"

"No, you're a woman. Transgender women are women."

"That's right, and who are they hurting by putting us down?" It killed me that I'd had to teach him that lesson. I didn't hide that I was a Trans woman. People assumed all the time because of my size. I'd spent too many years ashamed of who I was, yet I also felt selfish sometimes that I'd made my fight my son's, too.

"Themselves. Because they're showing their ignorance. We're lucky to have each other."

"Because..."

"We're each other's home." I cupped his face in my hands. I loved him so much.

"That's right, no matter where we go, who we're around, you are my home. We chose each other. You were born to be mine; another woman may have birthed you but..."

"I was always your son because the universe said you needed the perfect gift."

"That's right."

"Am I in trouble?"

"How many punches did you throw?"

"Maybe five."

"Five days of no video games. You're trained to defend yourself, love. That wasn't a fair fight." I'd put him in self-defense classes the day after he'd moved in with me. Not only was he a bit small for his age, but I was also his mother, and I wanted him prepared.

"Felt good, though."

I rolled my lips between my teeth as he leaned in close to whisper that.

"Violence never solves anything." Well, that wasn't true, and we'd already discussed defending ourselves. The situation warranted me not telling him I was proud he stood up for himself, but I didn't want him to fight because of me. I straightened and turned to find the two men who I assumed were the dads of the two boys looking highly uncomfortable, but Drake seemed to be paying too much attention to some file on his desk.

"You may speak now."

"We have a zero-tolerance policy for bullying and fighting. Each boy has earned a three-day suspension. The boys will be working with one of our counselors when they return to work out whatever issues."

"So, two against one, and my son gets suspended?" I shot a glare at the two men, and they snapped their mouths shut.

"He did throw punches, Sar—Ms. Hampton, fighting means suspension. You may come to the school daily to pick up his assignments. I can't show favoritism. A fight ensued. And I know at their age some people would prefer leniency, but they need to learn actions have consequences."

"Fine. Were apologies exchanged?"

"Yes, if unwillingly." Drake's voice said he wasn't happy about them not wanting to apologize as he looked at the other two boys.

"Can we go now?" I asked as I turned to start gathering up Reggie's coat and backpack.

"Please, Ms. Hampton, remain behind. I've already spoken to Mr. Danford and Mr. Cloister. I would just like a word with you for a moment."

"Fine. Reggie, wait outside, and I'll be right there." I ushered him out after I made sure the two men and their sons were gone. My son closed the door, and I turned back to the desk. "You had something to say?"

"Is Reggie receiving counseling?"

"Why? Because he has a fag in a dress for a mother?"

"Sari." His tone was sharp. "That's not what I meant. And I don't appreciate your defensiveness."

I pushed aside my moment of regret and held onto my anger and irritation. "Oh, you don't appreciate it. When my son had to defend us to two close-minded boys who probably learned to hate at home?"

He let out a heavy sigh. "Listen, I can control what happens inside these walls, but I can't do anything about what happens at home. If they came to school with bruises or injuries, I could call social services. But I can't get the authorities involved because the families are stupid. I just asked about counseling because I've noticed some issues."

"He goes to counseling once a week. He grew up in foster care, shuffled around for five years before he came to me. His adoption became final a few weeks before school started. He has some abandonment and stability issues. He doesn't form attachments like he should as he grew up knowing everything was temporary. No amount of counseling will fix that, it's a matter of trust and safety, and he still has a long way to go. I let him talk it out, and I respect his feelings. I was him for eighteen years. My last two years of high school were in a group home where it was survival of the fittest. *Lord of the Flies* was a fairy tale in comparison."

"I'm sorry."

"Nothing to be sorry for. I was an effeminate Black gay boy, an in-the-closet Trans woman just trying to survive until I could escape and be me. I'm honest with my son. He knew that he would probably get some bullying once they met his mother. I was told the community was inclusive, but even in safe havens, there's danger."

"I would've rather not have suspended him, but I can't—"

"You can't let one person get out of following the rules."

"Again, I apologize he was hurt. Um, he said he had worse?"

"He had foster parents right before he came to me…he still had the bruises. Seems the foster father didn't think he was tough enough, so he let his biological and foster sons beat up on Reggie to…toughen him up. There's a lot of loving foster homes, people who do all this for the right reasons, and the bad is usually the minority. But let's just say even a small minority of hatefulness is too much."

"I was told he has a helluva left jab."

"He started self-defense training at an MMA gym that an old friend owned the day after he moved in. He could've done a lot more damage if he wanted to."

"Don't think I didn't hear him say *it felt good, though.*"

The sudden smile curving his perfectly formed lips hit me right in the stomach. Dammit, that was not happening; I wouldn't allow it.

"I have no idea what you're talking about, Mr. Pike. Can I take my son home?"

"Of course, I'm sorry he had to defend himself. We'll definitely have an assembly on bullying."

"Thanks."

"I'd do it for anyone of my students who was being picked on.

You may have thought I was an asshole the first day of school, but I assure you, I was having a weak moment."

"I'm not so sure of that, Mr. Pike."

"Well, then I assume we won't be friends then."

There was that maddening smile again. "Probably. Good evening, Mr. Pike."

"You, too, Ms. Hampton."

I exited his office and collected my son. "Am I really grounded, Mama?"

"No, we just had to keep up appearances while we were in there. What do you want for dinner?"

"Pizza?"

He batted his pretty blond lashes at me, and he knew he had me. When I was on deadline, he ran the house. "We can stop and pick up pizza. But, baby, I don't want you fighting. I know you can protect yourself, and I signed you up so that I knew you could, but try to leave your MMA days for well into the future."

"Fine. I'll tell a teacher or Mr. Pike."

"Good, thank you." I kept the words as light as possible even as I wanted to order him not to talk to Mr. Pike. Reggie needed to keep his adorable nose clean because I needed as much distance between me and the sexy principal as I could get. Time to get my boy his pizza and some ice cream; Mama needed ice cream.

4

DRAKE

Five weeks into the school year and everything was uneventful, and I liked it that way. The holidays would be coming up soon, which meant after-school activities such as plays and all that. We'd have the Winter Carnival, which they always talked me into helping with because, you know, I didn't have a wife and kids. Of course, I had the time to deal with it.

I'd just walked out of the hardware store since my house was turning into a money pit, but I'd gotten a good deal on the old Victorian five years ago. I just didn't think I'd still be working on it. My gaze instantly landed on bright colors and a lemon yellow headwrap. The brighter the colors, the more Sari liked them, and you couldn't miss her. I'd started to live to catch sight of her picking up Reggie every day just to see what she was wearing. I checked the street and jogged across it and into the park where she sat on a bench.

"Ms. Hampton."

"Mr. Pike."

"Where's your shadow?"

"He's over there. He started Tai Chi after he came to live with me, and his heart was broken when he couldn't go to the park, and look what we found."

I followed the direction she motioned to find Reggie expertly following along with the others in the small group. He was the only person not older than their forties, but he seemed completely at ease.

"He seems really good."

"This, meditation, yoga, I might have a budding Buddhist on my hands. You can sit and not loom over me."

"Sorry." She waved off my apology as I sat down beside her. This was the first time I saw her outside the school setting. "Reggie said you're a writer. How did you get into that?"

"I was a journalist for a while, investigative for almost ten years. Got a bit dangerous, and with me wanting to foster and hopefully, eventually adopt, well, I had to make changes. I do freelance stuff for several online websites and magazines, mostly opinion pieces and the occasional advice column. And no, I will not tell you what my name is for the advice columns. The romance stuff came around when I was getting drunk to celebrate an award I received, and my editor dared me to write a romance. That was seven years ago."

"So, you've been a professional writer for seventeen years?"

"Yes. Are you trying to do the math, Mr. Pike?" Her full lips tugged into a half-smile, and I couldn't help returning it.

"Please, call me Drake."

"I'm flirting with forty but isn't there a rule not to ask a lady her weight or age?"

"I didn't ask. You offered." She was a decade younger than me.

She rolled her pretty eyes at me. She was a beautiful woman; I'd thought so since she walked into the classroom on the first day of school. We didn't get many new people to town, and since I didn't recognize her, I'd correctly assumed she was the mother of the transfer student. I took an interest in the new kids' well-being to make sure they settled into my school.

"How did you become principal?"

"It might not be a surprise, but I played high school football, but intellectually I understood my body wasn't going to hold out forever, and playing professional ball didn't interest me. I took my scholarship, went, and played in college. And while there, I got my master's in education. Moved back home after college, started teaching here, and became principal several years ago. In hindsight, I should've remained a teacher."

"Why's that?"

"I don't know. You deal with a good bit of politics as a teacher but nowhere near what I have to do now. I'm sure it's worse at the high school level, but..." I liked my job. I just didn't know how to explain my frustration with it sometimes.

"You seem well-respected. Reggie likes you, and he doesn't like anyone easily. He even talked to you the first day. I was surprised."

"I'm good with kids. You need to be with the job."

"None of—"

"Drake, honey." My mother's voice cut off the question I knew Sari was going to ask, and I was equally annoyed and relieved. Sari looked over my shoulder, and her smile brightened.

"Mom." I turned and saw Lanie Pike approaching in her flowing pink dress and her long silver hair pulled back into a ponytail. My mother was sixty-eight but looked younger than me most days. When I stood and opened my arms, she walked into them. Her head didn't even reach my sternum. "I thought you and Dad were away for the weekend."

"We'd planned on it, but a pipe busted at Davina's place, and with four kids, water is a requirement. Who's your friend?"

Dammit, I knew that expression, and she turned to Sari. The woman stood and held out her hand. I loved how tall she was. The top of her head would perfectly fit in the crook of my shoulder when I hugged her. I shook off the thoughts.

"Lanie Pike, this is Sari Hampton. She's the mother of one of my students."

"Oh." Her disappointment was clear. I always had the rule of never dating one of my student's mothers, and she knew I never broke one when I made it. "You're new in town."

"Yes, only moved here a few weeks before school started."

"Mama, Mama, did you see—" Reggie skidded to a stop and leaned against Sari's legs. "Sorry, I didn't mean to interrupt."

"Such a polite young man. I'm Lanie. I'm Mr. Pike's mother."

Reggie waved shyly.

"How are you finding our community?"

"It's nice. Definitely quieter than we're used to after living in the city. Still adjusting, actually."

"Are you and your son finding friends?"

"We're a little behind on that one. But I work from home, and Reggie—" She looked suddenly uncomfortable and went silent.

I knew Reggie had a few friends at school, but I didn't think they'd invited him places with them. They hadn't had another incident like the fight since I'd called an assembly when the boys had returned to school.

"You'll have to come over for Sunday dinner. He can spend time with my grandkids. Most of them are a little older, a few younger than Reggie, but I'm sure he'd have fun playing with them. He's probably already met a few of them at school."

"We don't want to be a bother."

"No bother at all. It'll be a welcome-to-town dinner. I was a stay-at-home mom when I wasn't working as a secretary for the family construction company. Hard to make friends when you work from home. Wait, you said your name was Sari Hampton?"

"Yes, ma'am."

"Oh my god, you're *the* Sari Hampton."

I chuckled at Reggie's loud groan, and he spun to lean on the back of Sari's legs. I sympathized because I tried to ignore my mother's obsession with romance novels, but I might need to check out her bookshelf or sneak and download one on my e-reader to see what Sari wrote.

"Yes, no one normally recognizes my name. I should've used a pen name, but I thought it would be a one-off situation. My agent appeared to think I was passable at writing it."

"I love your books, but I won't embarrass you. Now, you really do have to come to dinner. My daughters-in-law and my girls recommended them to me."

"If Mr. Pike doesn't mind. I don't want to intrude."

My mother turned to me and gave me the mom-glare. I knew what she was doing. She jumped on the opportunity to play matchmaker, something I never allowed her to do in the past. Normally, I would've put my foot down no matter what when she'd tried, but with Sari, she tempted me to let Mom do her thing. I didn't know what it was about Sari, yet I wanted to make friends at least. And from our limited interactions, I needed all the help I could get.

"I have no problem with it at all. I think you'd get along well with the ladies."

I earned a glare over my mother's head, and I put on my most charming smile. Sari's friendly smile returned when my mother turned back to her.

"Excellent. I'll leave you with Drake to get the details. Give her and Reggie a ride. It would be gentlemanly."

My tiny, adorable mother wouldn't let me defy her. She said her goodbyes and headed off in the direction of the hardware store.

"Is there any way at all, and I mean *any way,* I could get out of this?"

"Did you see her?"

"Yes, and she's scary, but she's your mother…you have inside intel."

"You happen to write crime novels?" The corner of my mouth ticked up as she snarled at me, and I wondered if she'd wear her hair natural like she had that first day of school.

"You're not funny or charming, Mr. Pike."

"Back to Mr. Pike now, are we?"

"Right now, yes."

"Reggie will have fun." I glanced down to find him leaning his slight body against her legs as she scratched the top of his head, mussing his sweaty hair. "And you can meet my two sisters and two brothers. My sisters and sisters-in-law have this standing ladies' night every Saturday. Me and my brothers and my sister's husbands watch the kids and do manly stuff like grill. Reggie can join the kids."

"I haven't even met them yet. How do you know they'll want to hang out with me?"

"Sunday dinner, no arguments. He'll have fun with the kids, and you can have a home-cooked meal and all the entertainment you want. We're a bit...insane. And if you need more incentive, my sisters love to torture me."

"What time?"

"Of course, that's what would get you. Want me to pick you two up?"

"No. We'll make our own way."

I could've argued with her. But I could see in her eyes that she wanted to have her vehicle in case she and Reggie had to leave if it turned into too much. She'd grown up in foster care until she aged out. Reggie had been in until she fostered and then adopted him, so family events could be hard for them. Her refusal hurt, but I could deal with that. I had to earn her trust.

"Give me your number, and I'll text you the address so you can use your GPS." I pulled my phone out of my back pocket, and instead of her reciting the number, Reggie did, and his mother shot him a look of utter betrayal.

"You need friends, Mama."

I laughed as she grabbed his hand and dragged him away.

"And you say you love me."

I chuckled behind them, not even offended that she didn't say goodbye, but I waved as Reggie twisted to wave at me. I just had to wait twenty-four hours before I could see her and her little sidekick.

5

SARI

I stood on the large porch of a beautiful older ranch-style home in a nice neighborhood. There were picket fences and perfectly landscaped lawns. I didn't belong there. My hands clenched around the plate with the cheesecake Reggie and I'd made that morning. Only a day had passed since I'd politely accepted the offer of attending a Sunday family dinner. When we'd pulled up, I'd almost drove right back off, but my son was looking forward to playing with the kids.

"Are we okay?" Reggie asked where he stood beside me.

"We're fine. It'll be okay. We're not used to family dinners, but we'll be fine."

"Do you think they'll like us?"

"They'll love you, love."

"They'll love you both." We both spun at the sound of Drake's voice behind us to find him on the top step. "You didn't have to bring anything."

"An internet search said it was polite to bring something." I felt my face heat.

"We're a big family, so it'll be appreciated. Have you knocked or just taking a minute?"

"Waiting."

"No need to wait." He smiled as he approached, and I tried to ignore how handsome he was.

I'd thought he was dangerous in his perfectly tailored suits, but after yesterday, him in jeans and a t-shirt was more so because he looked so much more approachable. I turned back to the door.

"Reggie, you can ring the bell," he said, and I tensed as a big hand spread across my lower back.

My sex life had taken a backseat to being a parent, but also, I'd never been comfortable with touch. For the first thirty years of my life, I was more used to waiting for the next hit or abuse because of who I was. That's why I'd avoided relationships, and I wasn't a fan of one-night stands, but...

My thoughts cut off as the door opened. An older man built on the same scale as Drake filled the doorway.

"Drake, you finally brought a date. Only took you fifty years."

The deep voice was thick with sarcasm, and I felt the corners of my mouth twitch, but it disappeared as Drake drew a slow circle on my lower back. I needed to put distance between us, but I didn't, only because I didn't want to appear rude. Or at least that's what I told myself.

"Nice to see you, too, old man."

"And who is this?" I liked the man the second he lowered to Reggie's level and held out his hand.

I stroked his hair to comfort him as he took the offered hand and gave it an awkward shake.

"I'm Reggie, sir."

"A young man with a strong, confident handshake and polite, we're going to be friends, but I think you're here to see my grandkids." He pushed up on his knees. "Too old to be doing that too much. I'm Draven Pike, and you must be the famous Sari Hampton. My girl has done nothing but talk about you since she came home yesterday." When he talked about his girl, his eyes twinkled.

"Sorry?"

Draven held out his hand, and I took it; I would've run from embarrassment as he turned my hand to bring it to his mouth to brush a kiss to my knuckles. If Drake's hand wasn't barring me from escape, I'd already be on my way back to my vehicle dragging Reggie behind me.

"Dad."

At Drake's sharp tone, Draven winked at me and slowly released my hand.

"Come on, young man, let's go see what the kids are doing."

I assured my son he was fine, and Reggie made his way into the house beside Draven. Drake motioned me forward and nudged me a little with his hand. I glanced over my shoulder to watch him close the door.

"You're welcome here. You know that, right?"

"I know I was invited, but we don't do stuff like this. We...it's always just the two of us."

"You'll do great. We can stand here a few minutes to let you prepare, but I assure you it's not scary unless you count my brothers, brothers-in-law, and dad arguing over the grill in the manly pursuit of grill master."

"You're not helping."

"Babygirl, I promise it'll be fine, but if it gets to be too much, none of us will judge you for leaving, neither of you." Compassion and understanding filled his bright, green eyes.

"I was never invited to anyone's home growing up."

"What about after you grew up?"

"Well, there were the college parties, a lot of alcohol, and... other stuff." He grinned. "I've gone to friend dinners, a lot of alcohol and other stuff. All my friends were professional people. No one had families yet or didn't want kids at all. I'd fostered for several years before Reggie was placed with me."

"He's an amazing kid."

Pride swelled in my chest at the knowledge I could say Reggie was mine. "He is, and I knew instantly he was mine."

"I overheard him being your home. If you don't mind me asking, what's that about?"

"Houses don't mean very much to me. It's just four walls and a roof over your head. I lost count of the ones I existed in. Home for me is where you belong...who you belong with. It's hard to find comfort with something you've never known. This isn't natural for Reggie, but he's still young enough to heal."

"You can belong here, too." He made the offer of sharing his family with me so easily. "My family is crazy and loud, pushy but loyal as hell. Ready?"

"I guess."

I tensed as he approached, and once again, his hand spread over my lower back, then he steered me toward the back of the house. "Babygirl, try to act like you're not being led to the volcano as a sacrifice."

"Good thing I'm not a virgin then." I laughed as he stumbled.

His sexy smirk made butterflies explode in my belly. "I knew we were going to be friends."

"I already told you, Mr. Pike, we're not friends."

"Going to be breaking my heart, babygirl?"

I didn't have time to respond as he took the pretty platter I'd bought specifically for the cheesecake and hoped my son and I didn't give anyone food poisoning. I stood back as he put it in the fridge.

"My son taking up all your time?" Lanie appeared through the sliding glass door that led to a deck.

"No, ma'am, he was just giving me a minute. He did talk about throwing me into a volcano."

"Drake, that's no way to treat a guest. No wonder you're single."

I snorted so hard I hurt myself and earned a glare. She took my arm and led me outside. I didn't have time to protest that I wanted to wait for him. As soon as we stepped out onto the back deck, I searched for Reggie.

"He's over there. He's fascinated with the boys and my husband debating the proper grilling methods."

"He'll play with the kids later."

"Don't worry about that. He can do what he wants. After we eat, the boys and the kids will play football. And the big kids will get their asses kicked. The tiniest girl, aka the con artist, will fake a hurt leg or a twisted ankle, there will be tears, and her other teammates will run the ball in for a touchdown. But because the big kids...they like to be called men...are gullible and don't know they're being conned in their panic. Happens every week."

I chuckled as she rolled her eyes and dragged me off to where a group of women sat. They all had wine glasses and were pointing and laughing at the men. I glanced at them to find Drake standing on the porch.

"Reggie, come get something to drink. Sari, what do you want? Beer? Wine? We have iced tea."

"Tea is great. I'm driving."

He nodded, and I watched Reggie run up the steps and inside with Drake. I turned back to the women, and Lanie introduced her daughters, Isa and Davina, and her daughters-in-law, Ria and Roxie. I sat down on an empty chair by Lanie.

"When's the next book coming out?" Davina leaned forward.

Ria pushed her. "Davi, let her get a drink first! But, yes, when's the next book coming out?"

"I don't know yet. I have to finish it first, and then my agent and company need to do their thing. It's the start of a new series. My company wants the entire book tour and signing."

"If you need someone to watch Reggie, we'd love to." Lanie offered. "Drake can take him to school, or he can go in with one of the grandkids."

"Don't let them bully you into anything, babygirl. Your iced tea, madam." He performed a gentlemanly bow, and I glared as I took the glass.

"Thank you," I pushed through clenched teeth.

"You better watch out. With that sweet tone of yours, you're going to give me ideas."

"I will sic my son on you, and I think he could take you."

He rolled his eyes. "My heart is overflowing. We're going to be friends one day. You can't deny me forever."

"I'm exceptionally stubborn, Mr. Pike."

"I have no doubt, Ms. Hampton. Let me go play referee and leave you ladies to gossip."

All the ladies in question except me flipped him off, and he walked away, letting out deep, rich laughter.

"That boy is getting too big for his britches." Lanie clucked her tongue.

"He's a pain in the ass," the other women said in unison.

"How are you finding our town?" Roxie asked.

"It's fine. I haven't seen much of it. Being on a deadline, I don't leave the house much. In the evenings, Reggie and I are unpacking, and we still have some stuff to get. We went from a smaller-sized apartment to a house."

"What brought you here? If you don't mind us asking." Lanie asked. All the women seemed to focus fully on me, and the strangeness of strangers paying me attention made me nervous.

"I don't mind. Reggie and I discussed it, and we wanted a house with a yard. I wanted an office that wasn't tucked into the corner of the living room, and he wanted a dog once we got settled. We signed the adoption papers a few weeks before we moved."

"What made you adopt?" Roxie asked.

"I always wanted a family." I turned to catch sight of him still hanging out with the men. "He'd been in foster care since birth. Healthy white children are the first adopted, so I was surprised when he came to me as a foster at five. But they noticed he was developing some behavioral and personality quirks. Long-term fosters sometimes become institutionalized, and with him getting older, he's less likely to be placed. When he arrived, I knew he was mine. He was barely with me a day before I called his caseworker. I figured since I had the kid, why not go ahead and get the house?"

"Well, you're more than welcome to send him to any one of us. We do a lot of overnights, ladies' nights, and one of us is always available for date nights," Ria offered.

"I don't date."

"Now, don't say that. You may meet a nice young man."

I shook my head at Lanie. "You mean that I'll meet a nice pain in the ass named Drake. Don't take this as an insult, but you're not very subtle."

"I've been told I'm very sneaky."

"I grew up in foster care and on the streets for a while, I know all the cons, and I can smell a setup from a mile away." When she'd invited me to dinner, I'd known what she was up to, and while I found Drake more attractive than I should, I wasn't prepared to date a man like him.

"He's not a bad-looking boy, a bit grumpy, but that's probably from lack of sex."

I nearly sent iced tea into my nasal cavity. "And his lack of anything isn't my business."

Draven saved me from more unnecessary information by yelling dinner. The men started herding the kids, but Drake stayed near Reggie, not letting the crowd overwhelm him. My chest tightened as I saw my son lean against the big man's legs, and Drake mussed his hair. I stayed back as well until everyone had their plates, and then Reggie and I went to the grill next to the table laid out with food enough for a professional football team.

"Help yourselves. Don't be shy, and we can find a spot to the side."

We didn't say anything while I made my plate and tried to do Reggie's, but Drake waved me off to find a spot for us. Shortly, the three of us were set off to the side, having dinner, and I was looking around. All the conversation and laughter. I'd seen scenes like this in movies, and I didn't feel like I belonged there. I wanted to run, but during dinner and the following football game where the men lost, Reggie seemed to be having a blast.

His sweaty hair stuck to his adorable face, his cheeks were flushed, and he had a big smile that showed off one missing tooth. I choked back tears at seeing him happy and included. We were kindred spirits. We understood that sense of never quite belonging. Seeing him surrounded by kids and Drake showing attention and patience as he explained the game or answered a hundred different questions, I finally felt like I'd made the right decision for us.

When the kids were ready to drop where they stood, Lanie ushered them inside to the living room where she'd made up a large pallet for them to sleep for the parents to collect them later. We all huddled around a fire pit for more drinking and conversation; so much laughter and love. What I'd seen all evening was what I'd dreamed of a family doing together. I was overwhelmed to be included, but it was also comforting in a strange way. Except for the daughters-in-law and Lanie, everyone was on the taller side. It was thrilling to *finally* fit.

"So, Sari, ready to run yet?" Draven asked from my right, but it wasn't a dig or contained any reproach for my introverted ways.

"Not run, but I really should be getting Reggie home." I stood up and turned to see Drake pushing up.

"I'll carry Reggie to the car for you."

"Thanks."

"Make sure you come back. Maybe next Sunday if you two want? We exchanged numbers, so we'll see if you'd like to maybe come out with us when you're done with your deadline." Isa gifted me with a friendly smile as she made the offer.

"Thank you. I may need it."

I suddenly realized Drake was gone, and I hurried into the house. I froze at the entrance to the living room. He carefully stepped into the maze formed by tiny sleeping kids. I watched as he crouched down to pick up my sprawled out and softly snoring son. He had Reggie safely cradled to his wide chest and made his way to me.

"I can carry him," I whispered.

"I got him. Go on before we wake up the other heathens."

I led the way out of the house and to my car parked a bit down the street. I opened the back door and stepped back, and watched him buckle Reggie in. He closed the door and turned to me.

"Was it painful?" he asked with a smile.

"No, no, it wasn't. And Reggie had so much fun."

"Well, you know how you can thank me?"

"I don't have sex on the first date." I smirked as he let out a loud burst of laughter.

"Wow, you think I'm that easy? Such a high opinion of me. I totally wait until the second date."

"Fine, what do you want?"

"Text me when you get home just to let me know you two are safe."

"What?" I stared at him, but I couldn't see much due to nothing but a streetlight. He was all in shadows.

"Text me once you're home and you have Reggie settled."

"O-okay."

"Thanks." He stepped back, and I didn't know what to say, so I made a run for it.

No one had ever asked me for a text or call, and except for my best friend, Janice, no one had ever worried about me. All the way home, I questioned why he wanted to know if I was safe. Yet the thing I didn't want to question too much was how warm and cared for his request made me feel.

6

DRAKE

I plopped down on the porch and leaned over to rest my forearms on my knees. When I'd told Sari to text me to make sure they were safe, her shock that I cared to mention it made me wonder what kind of friends or men she'd had in the past. All evening, I'd relived the moment we'd stood outside the door, my hand on her lower back, and how I'd felt like just the right size. I hadn't hunched or drew myself in so I'd appear less threatening.

"You're out of your league with that one."

I flipped my brother, David, off over my shoulder, and he chuckled. I groaned as my dad took the seat on the other side.

"Am I in for an intervention? Tell me I have no chance? Too pretty for me?"

"Son, you were out here a long time. Go in for the kiss and get shot down?"

I didn't know if I wanted to admit how much I'd wanted to lean in for a quick kiss, to see how well her tall form fit mine. Her mouth had looked so soft and inviting, and I wondered if she rushed off because she noticed my unwanted attention.

"No, I'd thought about it. I just told her to text me after she got Reggie to bed. She was shocked."

"You're going to have to be patient with that one, son. She has some pretty high walls built. She looks as if she's always on guard."

"I know. That's why I didn't fight Mom too much when she went in for her usual matchmaking. I need all the damn help I can get with Sari. Badly enough that I let Mom do her thing."

"From what Mom told me, you didn't fight at all."

"I thought we had the unbreakable rule of never dating one of the student's moms?"

"I was in Reggie's homeroom on the first day of school when they arrived. I'd never been tempted until that moment."

"What are you going to do about it?"

"I don't know, Dad. Make friends. Show her and Reggie around town. Get her to go out with the ladies for a night."

"Just tell us what you need, and we'll make it happen. But maybe see if you can talk her into a one-on-one outing. You can bring our soon-to-be grandson here for us to watch."

"You're getting a bit ahead of yourself."

"Your mother doesn't think so." Dad kissed my temple and got up to go back inside.

That was something I'd always noticed about my parents, especially my dad—he made sure we knew affection wasn't a sin. Even at forty-nine, I still got forehead kisses. It was odd when we'd compared our dad to others. We'd grown up to never hide our emotions; men cried, and there wasn't any shame in that outlet. Sometimes I thought that was why my relationships never lasted. You grow up with an example of parents who were married since eighteen and were as in love fifty years later, how could you find something that compared?

I wanted that with the woman I found. I preferred to be at home with whoever I dated. I didn't need bars or excitement. I just wanted a peaceful life, a wife and children. But at my age, I'd given up on that dream. My relationships weren't disastrous; I'd remained friends with a couple of my exes.

"You got that look. What are you thinking about?" David asked.

I glanced at him and tried to come up with an answer that wouldn't make me sound pathetic, but there wasn't one. "Why I can't keep a girlfriend."

"Don't even go there."

"Man, look at you and our siblings. Married with kids. You're doing all those things I wanted." I'd had a lot of time to analyze what I'd done wrong, and again, I was clueless, and nothing I said would make my family understand.

"Wanted? Why is that in the past tense?" He sounded disappointed.

"I'm almost fifty."

"You act like you're over the hill. You having one of those midlife crises that men have?"

"I don't think so." I knew when some men reached my age, they went crazy with recapturing their youths. Yet, I'd never viewed myself as a man who'd lose my mind over age.

"Mom and Dad gave us a damn near impossible example to live up to. Think about it, half a century together, and the longest they've ever been apart was two weeks when we gave all the ladies that cruise about five years ago. Dad still looks at Mom like he did when we were kids. Yeah, they fight. It takes work from both sides. You can't be the one to take care of everything or put in all the effort to make it last. You like Sari, don't you?"

"I shouldn't."

"Why not?"

"It's nothing bad. But you know I have a strict rule about dating a student's mother. Shit gets complicated, and kids get hurt. But the first time I saw her and Reggie...out of all the mothers I've seen interacting with their children...there was a bond that went way beyond what I'm used to. It was two kindred spirits who had connected. They'd chosen each other. They told each other they were each other's home. She grew up in foster care her entire life. She has no idea what family is. Reggie was in care before they'd placed him with her. It's that complete confidence, an unwavering bond between two people who were complete strangers almost two years ago. She said the minute she saw him, she knew he was hers."

"You want to be included in that bond?"

"Very much. But I don't think she trusts me or sees me like that. She's beautiful."

"Then do the friends thing like you said. Let her and Reggie get to know you. If nothing else, you made a new friend who you can secretly lust after."

"You're an asshole."

"Nothing new there. Drake, you already made an impression by asking her to text. Doesn't seem like something a man has asked her before."

"Shit, I left my phone—" The sound of something sliding across the porch from the front door. I glanced over my shoulder to find my sisters and sisters-in-law grinning at me.

"Your girlfriend texted to say she got home safe and that she had fun."

"Quit looking at people's messages."

"We were hoping it would be something juicy. It's been too long since you've gotten laid. Don't yell at us. Sexual frustration does that to a man. Also, you have to keep her around...there's gotta be perks to having a famous author as a sister-in-law. We need this, man." Davi fussed at me as the rest of the ladies held their hands together in a prayer pose.

I flipped off the giggling ladies as they slammed the door.

"I think they've gotten more annoying. Shouldn't they have mellowed out by now?"

"Have you seen Mom? There's no mellow in our genetics, and our wives are corrupted by association. It's been a long time since you've liked a woman. There was that, what was her name, Ellen, from two years ago, you dated her for about a year or two? We thought that had promise."

"She was divorced, and her kids were grown. She wasn't ready to settle down again. We had fun dating, but it wasn't going anywhere. I tried a one-night stand a year ago when I went to that educators' conference."

"You, a one-night stand? Man, you've never had a one-night stand in your life, not even in college."

"What's wrong with that?"

"Nothing's wrong with that. Quit being so defensive. You've never been so touchy about this shit before."

I scrubbed my hands over my face and over my two days' growth of beard. "Sorry. Let's get back inside and see about getting the kids loaded up."

"You know if you ever need to talk, we're there for you."

"I know. I appreciate it. I just have to figure out the best way to approach her."

"You'll work it out."

I nodded, and he got up to head inside. I twisted to grab my phone and woke it up.

Sari: *I got Reggie in bed. We're home and safe. Thanks so much for tonight.*

Sari: *Thank everyone for including Reggie. He had fun.*

Drake*: You're welcome. I'll tell everyone. Goodnight.*

I had sent the message and wanted to do a follow-up one to see if she wanted to have drinks some night. Instead, I stood and went to help get the kids in the cars. No matter my impatience to spend time with her—with them, she needed slow so that's what I'd do. No matter how much I hated it.

7

SARI

*S*hit, *shit, shit!* I paced my office and tried to figure out a plan. Janice wanted to meet with me in the city because she didn't want to meet in the middle of nowhere. I'd told her I wasn't living in some rural area with horror movie *Hills Have Eyes* potential. She'd refused. So, I needed to go to her to review the new contracts. She'd renegotiated the terms for the eight-book deal. It was more money than I'd made in all my years of writing fiction. It came with a book signing tour. I couldn't mess up my opportunity.

I picked up my phone, and I dialed the first person I could think of—Drake. His cell phone went to voicemail, so I hung up and dialed the school office, and the school receptionist answered.

"Yes, I'd like to speak with Mr. Pike, please."

"May I ask who's calling?"

"I'm Sari Hampton, Reggie Hampton's mother."

"Please hold."

I groaned at the sound of boring hold music with a mix of school announcements. Rolling my eyes, I waited.

"Sari, is everything okay?"

"Yes, I have a bit of an emergency."

"Are you okay?"

The concern in his voice did weird things to me, and I didn't want to analyze what that meant. "Yes, yes, my agent called. She wants me to come into the city this afternoon. The publishing company wants to talk about tours and new contracts. I tried to put it off, but the executives we're dealing with are going out of town and—"

"Babygirl, take a deep breath. Come on, just one."

I did as he asked and exhaled audibly, and he told me to repeat the deep, even breaths.

"Good girl. Do you need me to watch Reggie? He'll have to hang out with me for about an hour. I have to go over a few things for the upcoming winter carnival, but after that, we can go to my place. He can help me with a few projects, I'll make him dinner, and I can put him in my guest room to sleep if you're not back yet."

"You don't mind?"

"Absolutely not. I'll text you my address, and I can pick up some pajamas from one of my many siblings."

"Are you sure?"

"Sari, he'll be fine, and I'll explain to him you had a meeting and that you'll pick him up. He'll be safe with me."

"I know. I didn't know who else to call and—"

"You're panicking again."

"I've avoided these things before, but my new upcoming series, they want to do things I'm not used to, and I've never gone anywhere without him before. What happens if I have to be away for one of the signings?"

"We'll figure it out when and if that happens. And if by some chance you have to be away, guess what, you have a lot of people who offered to babysit. Yet I'll call dibs. They already have kids to hang out with, and I'm a bit jealous. I don't get enough favorite Uncle time."

"Okay, okay, I'm just not good at change. Make sure he doesn't have any homework to do."

"I'll make sure to check to see if he has any worksheets or reading to do."

"Thank you."

"Don't worry about it. Just take care of what you have to do, and Reggie and I will do manly things. I could use some help painting. That's all I had planned for the night."

"Painting?"

"I bought a house to fix up, and I've been doing a little at a time. I'll give you a tour if you're not too late getting home."

"Okay. I have to go through my garment bags for something to wear. You don't think sleep shorts and a tank top would work?"

His deep chuckle sent a shiver along my spine. "I don't think so. Get prettier than normal, and I got the kid handled."

"Thank you again."

"No panicking. You can call me any time. When you come tonight, I'll give you everyone's number in case something happens and you can't get me."

We exchanged goodbyes. I wasn't used to someone being so helpful. Yes, I had friends, but most of them were single or weren't parents, and they preferred the perks of aunt or uncle status for a limited time. Calling them would've meant them saying they were going to dinner or they had other plans. They had their own lives, but if I asked, they'd watch Reggie. Yet, I knew it wasn't something they were altogether comfortable with. In some ways, we'd grown apart as I'd had to cancel invites; told them I didn't have a babysitter or was on deadline.

Partying had lost its appeal long before Reggie came into my life. I preferred to write during the day and spend my evenings with Reggie, cooking dinner and getting him ready for bed, then a show or two before I read him a bedtime story. Why would I want to do anything other than my dream come true? Although, this was my first babysitter emergency. The fosters I'd had were all teenagers and able to watch themselves or go to a friend's house.

Reggie had friends from school he talked about, but he didn't get invites. A part of me felt guilty and wondered if it was because of me. I didn't want to think the worst about people or feel shame for who I was. I'd worked a long time to accept being a Trans woman and fought through all the obstacles of adopting.

I'd have to do something nice for Drake for agreeing to watch Reggie. Should I offer money? How much was babysitting worth?

I cursed as I realized I was procrastinating. I rushed for my room and the pile of garment bags that held my dressier clothes. After thirty minutes and that many mind changes, I found a bright orange, sleeveless dress that looked great against my dark skin, and I had a t-shirt turban to match. My curls needed more attention than I had time for. Black stiletto boots and a trench coat to finish it off, and it would have to do.

After a quick shower and makeup, I was presentable. *Fuck, I hated clothes*. Too quickly, I was in my vehicle and headed toward the city. I didn't want to do the hour commute, but hopefully, that would be the last meeting I had to do in person. Janice was usually the go-between. Eccentric, hermit writer worked well for me.

I'd made sure to text Reggie to let him know what was going on so he wouldn't feel insecure. He hid it well, but my boy had a bit of separation anxiety. He'd get my message as soon as school was over, and he turned his phone on. I knew it wasn't normal for a six-year-old to have the latest phone, but I wanted him to have a way to call or video call me at any time.

I took a deep breath as I passed the town limit sign and started the pep talk all the way to my meeting. The meeting, a quick dinner with Janice, and then home to my boy. I could survive that—maybe. The trip gave me too much time to think, and what subject did my brain want to focus on? The way too sexy Drake.

He was intelligent, nice, and handsome. I liked how tall he was. The roundness of his belly. It was more noticeable in his casual clothes than the tailored suits he'd worn for work. His baritone was a strange mix of gravelly and smooth. His forearms were hairy, and I imagined the rest of him was just as furry. I groaned as I pushed the thought of the unattainable man naked out of my head.

Focus on work and not on a sexy man who was completely off-limits. Finally, I made the trip through the city to Janice's office to ride over to the publishing house office together. Just a few hours and I could go home.

8

DRAKE

When I glanced at the clock, I saw it was almost ten PM. I'd sent text messages throughout the evening to make sure she knew Reggie was fine, and I'd tucked him into bed at nine after reading him a book we'd picked up from the library before going to get a pair of pajamas from Ria. After we'd done his spelling words for the next day, I'd put one of my t-shirts on him that fell all the way to the floor, and the short sleeves ended in the middle of his forearms. We'd tackled painting one of the guest rooms. More me than him, but he had a blast and posed for a bunch of pictures for his mom.

I collapsed on my couch after taking a shower and picked up my phone to see a text from Sari.

Sari: *I've never missed a bedtime before*

I'd smiled at her crying emoji. She'd complained all night and even mentioned Reggie not missing her at all. I'd shaken my head at reading that. Reggie was an amazing kid. Exceptionally bright and well-adjusted. But he'd insisted on video calling Sari to make sure she knew he was okay before she went in for her meeting.

I didn't know what it said about my life, but I'd had a blast taking care of him. Showing him the house, and he'd been concerned how lonely I'd be in such a big place by myself. Sari had done an outstanding job with him. It had taken him about an hour to relax, though. He was concerned about messing up, and I'd assured him there was nothing I couldn't fix.

Sari: *Stopped for gas and coffee. 30 minutes away.*

Drake: *Just be careful. We'll be here.*

I waited for another message, but when one didn't arrive, I stretched to reach the remote on the coffee table. Something to watch would pass the time. I didn't like her driving so late. She'd been awake since at least seven AM. Did she have a glass of wine? Did it make her tired and that's why she needed coffee?

Dammit, no wonder I couldn't keep a girlfriend. I worried too much. Did I stifle them with my need to take care of them? I didn't remember being this attracted to a woman before. I loved her snark and how she easily gave me shit. There was still no clear plan on how to get her to see me as a former adversary and a budding friend. When she'd called me that afternoon, I'd felt shocked she'd trust me with Reggie. I hadn't taken her faith lightly.

Frustrated that nothing held my attention except thoughts of Sari, I tossed the remote aside and pushed up off the couch. I'd grab a cold beer and hope it helped me to relax; I hadn't slept great lately. Opening the fridge, I picked up one of the three bottles left. I didn't normally drink at home. I might buy a six-pack once a month. I closed the door and twisted off the top as the doorbell chimed.

I looked down at myself in workout shorts and a white tank—good enough. Setting the bottle on the island I'd added when I'd remodeled the kitchen, I walked through the house. Luckily, I'd renovated the first floor the first year living there, and I was halfway finished with the second, but the third floor was a construction zone.

When I opened the door, I froze. She had a bright head wrap around her mass of curls and wore a trench coat over an orange dress. I loved how bright she was; she didn't try to minimize herself to fit. Her confidence drew me more than anything. I shook my head and invited her in. Then I offered to take her coat. She started to protest but allowed me to slip it off after she released the knotted belt.

"You look beautiful. How was your meeting?" I rushed to ask how her evening was.

"It was good. Janice made sure that if can stick to my deadlines and don't get distracted, I'll be able to pay my bills."

"That's always a good thing. You want something to drink?"

"No. I just finished my coffee. Was he good for you?"

"Perfect. He got more paint on him than the wall, but he had fun. That's all that mattered."

"This house is amazing."

"Thanks. Before I moved in, I did all the work on the first floor, and Dad did all the rewiring. That's not my strong suit. I lived in what I guess would've been the library until I finished a bedroom. Second floor is still a bit of a construction zone. You want a tour, or do you have to get going?"

"A tour would be great. I'm a bit of a night person, and the coffee didn't help."

I led her through the living room, a formal sitting room, and the library with floor-to-ceiling shelves. I counted the click of her heels on the hardwood floors and tried not to stare at her. I stood back as she walked around the large room. Most of the books on the shelves came with the house.

"This room is amazing. I've never seen a library in a house. Seems like a lot of room for one person."

"Took forever to refinish the shelves. I got an amazing deal on the house. It was sitting empty for a decade as the family fought over the estate of the old man who owned it. It turned into a bit of a money pit. The plumbing and electric had to be completely updated before I could move in. We used to think the house was haunted when we were kids."

"Is it?" I caught her smile as her fingers stroked over the ornate wood paneling, and I suddenly wanted to know what her fingertips felt like on my skin. How would that beautiful smile feel under my lips?

I cleared my throat as I tried to rid myself of my dangerous thoughts. "No, just housed an old, lonely man with family just waiting for him to die."

"That's grim."

"It was, but unfortunately true."

"I'm not an expert, but everything looks beautiful."

"Thanks. Years of working for my dad's construction company came in handy." I led her to the kitchen.

"A lot of fireplaces." I let her take everything in. Then we headed for the stairs. "We had one at the apartment, but it was more for show than use."

"I thought about sealing them up because they're not necessary now, but I wanted to keep it as original as possible. It does help with heating costs, though."

"That bill has to be brutal. What do you have left?" she asked.

"I did all the wood refinishing on all floors. There were some rotten planks on the hardwood floors, so those all needed replaced. Second floor just needs painting now. I lucked out a bit because they sold everything in the house that wasn't an antique. So a lot of the furniture I got to keep. Just needed some TLC. Reggie's in that room." I pointed at the only guest room that I'd finished other than the one I slept in. "The door next to it is mine."

"What about the third floor?"

"I broke with tradition on that one. Come on." I felt her behind me as I went to the staircase at the end of the hall that led to the third floor. "This one is going to be my bedroom when it's done. I had to do a redesign to add a bathroom. I took out the walls and added pillars. When I purchased the house, I thought I'd have to stick with some rules, but I found out it hadn't been deemed historical, which meant I didn't have to follow protocol. The double doors lead out onto a large balcony that overlooks the yard. David is the landscape person, so he's going to take care of all that when I get around to it. There's a fountain that needs repaired. He can fix that, too."

"You have a beautiful home. I was a little intimidated when I pulled up."

"Why?"

"These were the types of houses we used to go by back in the day and imagine the lives on the inside."

"What was that like?"

"I was envious. The homes I lived in were nothing like this. Small houses in overcrowded neighborhoods. I didn't even have my own room until I rented my first apartment."

"I know some homes are good, but was it bad for you?"

"No...not really." She opened doors, checked out the bathroom, and then walked out onto the balcony. I followed. "My file said I went into care after a few weeks in the hospital. The little information that was in my records said my mom was barely eighteen. In a way, I thanked her for giving me up. People who aren't ready for kids shouldn't keep them."

"Ever look for her?"

"No. I don't know if I'd remind her of something she'd rather forget. I went into a never-ending series of foster homes after that. People move. They have biological kids. Life happens. At fifteen, I ran away, was on the streets for about a year and a half. State-run groups homes aren't always the safest place for kids like me. I took my chances."

"Time ran out?"

"Yeah. I pocketed some cupcakes one night we were going to celebrate one of our friend's birthdays, and the owner of the store caught me. Called the cops. In the end, he didn't press charges, but I was back with the state. My caseworker, man, he was an asshole, but he genuinely cared about the cases that came across his desk. He told me what I did with my life was my choice and asked if I wanted to end up in jail or have a nice life one day."

"Am I safe in assuming you made the nice life choice?"

"Not at first. I liked giving him shit."

I loudly laughed at her mischievous grin. "So, nothing has really changed."

"Not really." She turned to lean against the railing to look at me. "I started going to school and paying attention. He used to show up every week. Hell, I never met a person so interested in me doing good. I think I'd been in the group home a year; it was hard, I was shy and effeminate, but I also had an attitude. He came to pick me up and took me to an LGBTQ teen support group. He worked at the center...him and his husband. He picked me up every Saturday to attend."

"Did it help?"

"Not at first, but I tried to butch up. Weakness made you a target. Did I apologize for my attitude in your office that day?"

"No need for that, babygirl. It's fine."

"Man, I pissed you off."

"No. I was already pissed, but I will admit the gay slur in a dress didn't help. I wouldn't view you or anyone else like that."

"I don't want my son to have to fight to protect me. We discussed that having a six-foot-two, Black mama wouldn't be easy. Kids don't think in terms of bigotry until they're taught to hate. In the city, it was easier. The school was inclusive. It was in a neighborhood that was right next to the queer section of the city."

"Was it hard to come out?"

"Yes, being a Black Trans woman isn't safe, and I'd always been extremely vocal about my activism. Let's just say doing a search of my name...you can find out a lot of information. Leaving the house sometimes is anticipating violence, but it was either accept who I was or pick the option a lot of Trans people take."

She didn't have to say what that option was, and I didn't want to know how many times she may have debated it.

"If I say something wrong or ask something too personal, all you have to do is say so."

"You're good. Not many women are my height, and, well, sometimes people speculate. It's a hazard of being me, but you've been nothing but nice."

"Not that first day, though."

"Want to tell me why I made you grumpy?"

"I've always been oversized, tall. I work out, and the house keeps me in shape. You looked scared of me."

"I'm sorry if I made you self-conscious."

"Thanks, but it's an old insecurity. Doesn't pop up as much now that I'm older. I learned the world isn't always accessible to tall people. And I know sometimes women don't feel safe with men my size."

"Why aren't you married? Or have enough kids to fill this place?"

"I've had several semi-long-term relationships, but they never worked out. The last one, she was divorced with grown children, and she had no urge to start over. Back in my twenties, I even thought I was close to marriage. We'd seemed on the same page."

"What happened?"

I approached her and turned to sit on the railing beside her. "I don't fully know." I crossed my arms over my chest.

"Defensive posture." She tapped my forearm and dropped her hand back to the railing.

"I don't mean to be. I guess it was more me than her. Mom and Dad set this horrible example."

"Horrible in what way?"

"They've been happily married for fifty years. They're not complacent. They're happiest together."

"Your siblings are married with kids." She pointed out.

"That's what David told me, too. I'm most like my dad. I'm

affectionate. I worry about the person I'm with. Like I asked you to text me the other night. Partying doesn't hold a fascination. I don't mind dates or going out with friends, but I'm happiest at home with my partner. I'm not a drinker. I get a six-pack here and there, once a month maybe."

"Doesn't sound too bad. My partying days ran their course before I was out of my twenties. Nothing wrong with that. We grow. Find out what works for us. My friends, as much as I knew they loved me, they didn't understand me wanting a family. I was successful in a job I loved. Had my own place. Freedom. We all have what we like."

"You always wanted kids?"

"Yes." Her smile was the brightest I'd ever seen it. I wish the lights were brighter so I could take it in better. "It was one of the only things I was sure about. But growing up, I never thought of it as a reality that I'd adopt. Then I met up with my old caseworker one night, him and his husband were at a restaurant where me and my friends were having dinner. He suggested becoming a foster parent."

"I thought about it at one time, too."

"You should. I think you'd be a great parent."

"Maybe."

"I better get Reggie and head home. I was out a lot later than I planned." She pushed up from the railing. "Thanks so much for watching him."

"Any time. I have that list of numbers in the kitchen with his backpack. You just need the guys' numbers. The ladies mentioned they already gave you theirs. Let's get Reggie, and I'll grab it for you."

We returned to the second floor, and I wanted to offer her a place to stay for the night but thought twice. I pushed open the door and let her go first. She eased the covers off her sleeping son, and there was that look again. Such happiness and peace; I'd seen it on my parents' faces when they looked at us.

"Let me pick him up. You need to put your jacket on. It's too chilly to go without it."

She nodded, and I picked him up—the boy was out.

Too quickly, I closed the front door behind them. I recognized my loneliness. It was something I'd accepted as I grew older and remained single. I didn't realize until they'd left how deep it was. I went back to the kitchen and poured out the warm beer.

Sleep and everything would be back to normal...I needed it to be normal.

9

SARI

I'd finished the first book ahead of my deadline, and to celebrate, Drake ordered me to bring Reggie to his place, and his sisters, sisters-in-law, and his mom took me out. Fighting with the man proved useless. The guys had taken all the kids to the park and then out to dinner at a place with an arcade and exceptionally unhealthy food. Afterward, they had set up tents in Drake's backyard.

Even if I'd thought about saying no, Reggie bounced with excitement to get to hang out and *camp* for the first time. He'd rushed me out of the house so fast he'd hurt my feelings.

"Don't take it so hard, Sari." Lanie gave me a tight hug.

"He just couldn't get rid of me fast enough."

"It happens. Ours used to be mama's boys, too, and then one day it hit, they wanted to be mini men. It's horrible." Davina shook her head and sipped her wine.

"Breaks aren't bad things. We enjoy our weekly ladies' nights. Get to dress up and put on makeup, have conversations that don't consist of fart humor or fights over bath time or that clean clothes are required, or clothes period, are required. D.J still refuses to wear clothes." Ria was rolling her eyes. "I had to sprint down the street last week to catch his little ass. A five-year-old shouldn't be faster than you. He was shrieking to wake up the entire neighborhood."

"You still haven't lived down the sheer curtains yet," Isa said with a snort.

"How was I supposed to know the three houses across the street had a clear view to their very own free nightly porn show. That little old grandma pointing it out was not embarrassing at all. And David, his annoying ass asking if they got him at his best angle."

I snorted into my wine and made a mental note not to drink around my new friends.

"Or let's not forget the always popular game of is this a booger or a remnant of a gummy in your hair." Isa shook her head.

"Come on, ladies, we're out. Let's not think about our kids and men." Roxie waved over our server and ordered another bottle of wine.

"Is someone having a lover's quarrel with their man?" Isa giggled, and Roxie flipped her off.

"Nolan is just being Nolan."

"Roxie had a lot of complications with their second, and Nolan doesn't want to try for another. They'd discussed having three before they got married." Lanie filled me in.

"The doctor says I'm perfectly healthy. They said there was no reason this one couldn't be like the first."

"Just give him time to process." Ria gave Roxie a hug, and the conversation ended as we ordered our dinner.

We shifted to lighter topics, and everyone asked if I was having a local signing because they all wanted to come to support me. I assured them that I'd let them know when Janice sent me a schedule. They made sure to let me know any of them would be up for babysitting.

"Drake offered if I needed to go out of town for a weekend. I told my agent that I needed a schedule where I wouldn't be gone for more than a few days at a time."

"Are you excited about a book tour?" Lanie asked.

"I don't know. It's all been going great. I have my freelance stuff, and I can go back to journalism if I need to, but I like being able to stay home with Reggie. I didn't know my proposal and sample of the first book would take off. This is so outside my comfort zone."

"It'll be amazing, and we'll be there to help with Reggie. My grandkids adore him, and Drake will watch him any time. Everyone needs a support system, and you have one."

"Thanks." I hoped they didn't hear my voice break, or if they did, they wouldn't point it out.

We sat there for hours, talking, laughing, and drinking too much wine. I was going to pay for that in the morning. It had been at least two years since I'd drank too much. Refraining hadn't bothered me because Reggie was always my top priority. Although, I had to admit, having friends that got the responsibilities of raising kids was nice.

"Ladies, our very sexy chauffeur has arrived," Roxie slurred.

I jerked my head up to find Drake standing at the head of the table, shaking his head. "No puking in my vehicle. I should've brought the truck. I could've just thrown all of you in the bed of it."

"We just have to pay our bill." Roxie fumbled her purse.

"No, I already took care of it. Time to deliver you to your homes where you can be miserable when your husbands and kids come home tomorrow."

I smiled as each woman picked an equally tipsy partner to lean on and I stood, stumbled a bit and a strong, bulky arm wrapped around my waist.

"Easy, babygirl. Lean on me. I'll make sure you get safely to the car."

"Where's Reggie?"

"Last time I saw him, he'd had way too many s'mores and had the giggles."

"Oh man, maybe you should—"

"Not a chance, babygirl. I'll bring him home in the morning after he's had breakfast. We already have plans, blueberry pancakes from Maggie's Diner and a trip to the hardware store. You'll have plenty of time to caffeinate. There's nothing worse than a wine hangover."

I groaned, and I shot him a dirty look when he laughed at my future pain. "We're not going to be friends."

"Too late, beautiful." He squeezed my hip as the cool, fall air hit my too-hot face.

I wasn't used to compliments from men just because. The last time a man paid me attention, it was to get me into bed, and there was no way, even with me drunk, I'd think a man like Drake was trying to fuck me.

"We left you shotgun, Sari," Isa yelled, and I looked up to find women crowding in the open back window. Davina was either sitting or standing to look over the roof from the driver's side rear.

"Davina, get in the damn seat before you fall out. Remember freshman year of college. Mom is still giving me dirty looks for those stitches." He griped at his sisters and mom to buckle up as he opened the passenger door and helped me into the seat.

I went to reach for the seatbelt, but he got to it first. He leaned into my space, and I could scent woodsmoke and chocolate along with some spicy cologne. I'd had too much to drink because I wanted to bury my face against his neck and just bask in the scent of him.

"There you go, all safe. Let's get the party animals home, and then I'll drop you off. Your place is on my way home." He told the women to shut up when they aww'd.

I didn't trust myself to speak, so I just nodded and relaxed into the seat. He moved around to the driver's side and started the process of dropping off his sisters and mom. His mom was the last one, and he carried her to the door, bracing her on his thigh as he unlocked the door. I leaned my head back and closed my eyes.

"No falling asleep yet. You have to get home, have some water and some medicine."

I turned my head as he slammed the door. "Did you tell all of them that?"

"Actually, I got them the pain relievers and water before I left."

"How did you get taxi duty?"

"It was my turn. Every Saturday night, one of us arrives wherever the ladies are, pays the bill, and gives everyone a ride home."

"That's really nice."

"Not really. Everyone works hard all week at their jobs. Taking care of their husbands and kids, always thinking about themselves last, so this is our way of letting them have time to have fun. No kids to worry about. No dinner to make. Then the morning after, they get a quiet morning to do what they want. Catch up on reading. Binge-watch something. Each Dad takes their kids to do something in the morning."

"And it's always been like that?"

"Yeah, it started with me when I was old enough to take care of the kids. Mom and Dad would go out Saturday night for dinner and get a hotel room. When everyone started getting married and having kids, we banded together. Now, it's a ladies' night."

"You have a very nice family. They said they'd come and be supportive at my first signing if it was nearby."

"Of course they did. My family likes you. You and Reggie fit right in."

"I always wanted a family like that." My eyelids drifted closed.

"You're welcome to mine, babygirl. We're almost home. Just stay awake a little longer." His slightly calloused hand cupped the side of my face and stroked over my cheekbone. His thumb tickled my lashes.

The SUV pulling to a stop woke me from my doze. When I looked around, he was already out and circling the front of the vehicle. He opened the door and offered his hand.

"Do you need me to carry you, too?"

"I think I can make it." I got out, and he instantly hugged me to his side as I searched my purse for my keys. I pulled out my phone and housekey, and I pouted as I saw no messages. "He didn't even message me."

"Babygirl, we kept them going the entire night. I have plenty of pictures he made me take so you could see. I'll send them to you when I get home, and you can look at them while you relax in the morning." He took my key and unlocked the door, and then he released me so I could enter the dark house. "You want me to get you settled before I go?"

"No, I'm fine. I'm going to get some water and take some pills, and then I'm going to take a long hot shower before bed."

"Sure I can't stay? I can wash your back and make sure you're safe in that hot shower." He smirked and winked at me.

"Go home, Drake, and take care of my boy. Thanks for the ride, and…thanks for everything."

"You're welcome." He placed my keys in my hand. "I'll wait here until I hear the door lock, and I'll be on my way."

I leaned forward to kiss his cheek, but I was off, and my lips landed on the corner of his mouth. "Goodnight." I panicked and slammed the door. Turned the deadbolt and turned to rest against the door.

"Goodnight, babygirl. I'll text in the morning."

I stood there with my eyes closed until I heard his engine start and the headlights disappeared. Only I could fuck up a cheek kiss. I kicked off my shoes as I passed the living room and headed to the kitchen for water and a couple pain tablets. The sooner I fell asleep, the better, but my anxiety would have me reliving that misplaced kiss for the next fifty years.

10

DRAKE

Drake: *Well, are you coming or not?*

I stretched out on my couch, waiting for Sari to respond to my text. It was Halloween, and as always, me and my siblings banded together to take all the kids trick or treating. We had a map of the best houses that gave out the good candy. Halloween was a big deal in the Pike family, and I wanted her and Reggie to come with us. We had two hours before we needed to be at David's house for Ria to do the zombie makeup. We were a zombie horde and would be *chasing* the kids from house to house.

Sari: *Getting a little impatient, Mr. Pike*

Drake: *YES! We have two hours*

Sari: *You're more excited than Reggie*

Drake: *Are you ready yet?*

Sari: *You're annoying*

I smiled at my phone, imagining her adorable eye roll. She'd become a regular for Sunday dinner and the ladies' nights, and Reggie was even spending nights with my nieces and nephews. I loved seeing them settling into town, but her and I hadn't had any one-on-one time since I'd dropped her off at her place. I wanted to ask if she'd avoided me because I said or did something wrong.

Yet, I didn't want to put her on the spot. I checked the time and saw ten minutes had passed.

Drake: *Are you ready yet?*

Sari: *You can come pick us up if you miss us that much*

I was off the couch, picked up my keys, and shoved my wallet in my back pocket. My costume was already at my brother's place.

Drake: *On my way*

Sari: *DRAKE!*

I ignored the message and made sure I'd turned everything off. Owning my house had one con—no one ever came there for trick or treating. Also, it didn't help I was on the edge of town on a hill. I got in my SUV and headed across town to pick them up. I cursed myself when I didn't ask if she'd dressed up. The ladies usually picked princess costumes—something with a cape to stay warm as we made the rounds.

It was only a fifteen-minute trip before I pulled in behind her vehicle. The door opened, and Reggie ran out. He wore a tiny business suit with a crooked tie and small glasses with tape around the nosepiece. I didn't know how much gel he had in his hair, but it was slick and shiny.

"Hey, Drake."

"Hey, Reggie. You ready to get all the candy?"

He nodded his head so quickly it knocked his slightly oversized glasses crooked. I closed my car door.

"Is your mama re—"

Holy fuck! Sari stood framed in the door. Her mass of curls were tamed into two braids over her shoulders. She had on a red dress with a deep V neckline that showed shallow cleavage. The hem fell to the middle of her thick thighs, and knee-high stiletto boots made her legs appear even longer.

"I hope you have a jacket or a cape to wear." Because she was too damn pretty. Her inherent sexiness kicked my possessiveness into ridiculous levels. I wouldn't be able to handle every man we passed hitting on her when I had no right to claim her.

"Yes, Red Riding Hood is a little cliché. She got catfished by the Big Bad Wolf in a Granny nightgown and bonnet, but I had all the pieces in my closet. You're not dressed up."

"Ria has my costume, and she needs to do all of our makeup. So, we're headed over there for a little dinner before we head out. You have everything?"

"Just a few minutes. I have to grab the cape, and I have a picnic basket for candy overflow and my wallet and phone. Come on in. Reggie, get your briefcase for your candy."

He ran inside, and she turned to the side to avoid getting run over.

"He seems excited."

"He's been looking forward to spending the evening with the kids. I was just going to meet everyone at your parents' since Davina said that was the first stop."

"Mom and Dad like to see all their adorable grandchildren dressed up before they get a sugar high. Now that I'm here, you can ride with me. Want me to grab his booster seat?"

"Yeah, that'd be great." She leaned inside, and I heard her alarm beep and the locks click.

I made myself busy moving his seat from her car to mine. Then I headed for the door. It stood open, so I entered without knocking. I bit back a groan as I walked in to find her bent over at the waist, fixing something on Reggie. The bottom of her dress exposed the cutest dimples in her upper thighs. I wasn't going to survive the night.

I gave myself a pep talk about not dragging her into the shadows while the kids were getting their candy. I got Reggie and her buckled in, then made my way to David's. He'd gone full haunted house even though they wouldn't be home to hand out candy.

"I heard there was a Pike Halloween Mission...sounds serious."

"We have a map of all the houses that give out all the good candy. We're talking full-sized bars and bags. No candy corn for our kids."

"You all take this thing seriously."

"It is. We don't play when it comes to candy, babygirl." I smiled at her husky laughter. I parallel-parked outside my brother's place. "Reggie, you can unbuckle and go in. The door's unlocked. I just need to get your mom out."

"I can unbuckle and open my own door. I've been doing it for a lot of decades now."

"Ha-ha, sit tight." I was surprised when she didn't reach to release her seatbelt. All she did was roll her eyes at me, and I slipped out as Reggie slammed the back door and took off running for the house. I watched him until he disappeared into the house.

I pulled the handle and opened the door. I leaned into her space and took in the femininely spicy perfume she wore; her hair smelled almost sweet. I took my time releasing her, letting my cheek stroke over hers. She gasped, and I felt the little puff of air. I caressed my fingertips across the cute curve of her belly, but I resisted the urge to test how soft it was. I straightened and offered my hand as I picked up the basket at her feet. My gaze fell to her full, red lips, but I got myself under control as I let go of her hand; only to spread my hand across her lower back. I carefully led her up the walkway, the steps, and into the house.

Wolf whistles came from my brothers and brothers-in-law. Instead of flipping them off like I wanted, I glared at them. My murderous expression only worsened as I removed her cape. I'd destroy them all later.

WE WERE on the last street on our map, and the kids started to lose some of their enthusiasm as they grew tired. Sari's basket was almost full of overflow from Reggie's briefcase. It was a smart move; they barely saw any candy in it and would sneak him a few extra.

"Are you doing okay?" I placed my chin on Sari's shoulder and whispered in her ear.

"Yeah, these boots were not made for trekking the entire town. You were not joking about this being important business."

"Told you." I placed my left hand on her hip and felt her tense a bit.

For most of the evening, I'd made sure to enter her personal space but retreat when I sensed it was too much. As the night wore on, she became more comfortable with my touch and presence. I wanted a kiss when I dropped her off at home.

"We only have four more houses. We made a circle of several neighborhoods, so we're only a few streets over from David's place."

We followed behind, waiting on the sidewalk as the kids ran up to ask for their candy. The adults weren't holding up any better than the kids. We'd finally reached the last house, and as we walked, I'd kept my arm around Sari's waist, her side pressed flush to mine. With her heels on, she was actually a few inches taller than me, and I loved it.

Reggie came running, a sleepy smile on his adorable face. I'd only just broken contact with Sari when Reggie handed me his briefcase and tucked himself between us, taking our hands. My chest tightened. We hadn't spent nearly enough time together, but I was positive I wanted to be included in this little family.

She trusted me with her son's safety, but I needed her to trust me with hers, too. I was determined to spend more time with them with the holidays coming up. She'd mentioned they weren't doing anything special, and they were already invited to my parents' place. Usually, the day of the holiday, I vegged at home with takeout while my siblings went to their in-laws, and the Sunday after was our celebration. This year, I was having it with Sari and Reggie at my house; I'd already planned everything out.

I glanced down and smiled as I saw Reggie almost asleep on his feet. I released his hand and bent to scoop him up in one arm.

"I can get him."

"He's fine. We're almost back to the car, and I can get you two home." I smiled at her as he looped his arms around my neck, tucking his face against my neck. His breaths quickly evened out, and he was asleep. I noticed my nieces and nephews weren't far behind.

I didn't miss that my family kept glancing behind them at us, and I saw the smiles. They kept offering to invite Reggie over so I could take Sari to dinner or just to have drinks. I knew she wasn't used to the attention, the requests for text messages, or when I opened doors for her. Again, I wondered about the people in her past. How did they not want to take care of her—make her happy?

We'd made it back to the house, and after quick goodbyes, everyone loaded up. She opened the back door, taking the case, and I put him in his seat. I took the case and basket to set them on the floorboard. As soon as I had her in the car, she let out a relieved sigh as the pressure was off her feet. I knew she preferred sandals or barefoot.

"I'll get you home in a few minutes, babygirl."

"My feet will thank you."

"You want me to rub them when we get home?" I smirked as she pushed against my chest.

Once I was in the driver's seat and pulling away from the curb, she spoke, "He had so much fun, thanks again. I always seem to be thanking you for something."

"You don't have to. I loved having you two along. I was wondering if you'd like to come to my house for Thanksgiving and Christmas. The day of is usually for the in-laws, and we get together at Mom and Dad's the following Sunday."

"You don't have anything planned?"

"Normally, I just get takeout, find something to binge-watch, and not leave my couch. Spending it with you two sounds like a lot more fun."

"I'd have to help cook. I'm not great in the kitchen, well, nothing that isn't six-year-old approved, but I think I can assist in making a holiday meal."

"Perfect. You can come over in the morning. We can do all the prep. Then we can veg together by watching TV and eat ourselves into a coma in the afternoon. You didn't have any plans?"

"My friends do a gourmet Friendsgiving. Nothing Reggie would want to eat. I'd have to get a hotel room because I wouldn't want to drive an hour home afterward."

"Your friends aren't married or have kids?" She'd mentioned some were married, but none of them had kids yet; it just seemed they'd make an effort to include Sari and Reggie.

"No. They love me, but they didn't understand me wanting to give up my life and freedom to become a mom at almost forty. I had a career. My apartment was too small but in an exclusive part of the city. When I didn't have a foster living with me, I traveled because I could, but often it was for research or some convention."

"I think you made a great decision."

"Appreciate it. It took a little over a year to get the judge to sign the paperwork, which isn't bad for an adoption. There's a lot of paperwork, home studies, social worker visits, but even if it had taken a decade, he was still going to be mine."

"What about a dad or second mom for him?" I glanced at her but couldn't make out her expression in the passing shadows between the streetlights.

"I've dated, but when you're a writer who barely leaves the

house, it's hard to find someone. I'm not one for those apps everyone swears by. Also, one-night stands hold no appeal. In the end, I decided to do something I could have some control over. Becoming a mom. To be honest, I never pictured anyone else with us."

"Well, it's different here. You have people to watch Reggie so you can go out." I didn't look at her as I pulled into her driveway and turned the engine off. I turned to take her in.

"Things have changed since I moved here, that's for sure."

"How so?"

"I met you and your crazy family. Reggie has a bunch of new friends. I have friends who get the mom things. I can go places and bring Reggie along, and they like having him there, not just tolerate him because he's mine."

"He's not something to be tolerated. He's always welcome."

She nodded. "I better get the boy inside, whether we like it or not, he has school tomorrow. Thanks for allowing us to participate in the Pike Candy Mission."

"You're welcome. You going to fight me about opening your door and carrying him inside?"

"Would it help?"

"No."

"Didn't think so."

Once I got them both inside, we spent time together at my place, so, she told me where his room was so that I could lay him down while she went to drop off the candy in the kitchen. When I made it back to the living room, she was waiting for me.

"This is where I tell you to text me when you get home."

"And I'll do it as soon as I park. Get some rest, and I'll see you tomorrow." I kept a distance between us because even though I'd thought about it all night, I didn't think I'd be satisfied with one kiss. I crossed to the door and opened it. "Babygirl?"

"Yeah?"

"You looked beautiful tonight."

She dropped her chin to her chest. Compliments still made her uncomfortable. I made sure to give her plenty, I didn't want to feel awkward, but I loved that beautiful, tiny smile too much.

"I'd say you looked handsome, but the gore is kinda gross." She grinned at me.

"Goodnight, Sari."

"Night, Drake. Be careful going home."

It took every ounce of self-control to walk out of her house. I hadn't wanted to leave. I wanted that first kiss; I didn't count the one she gave me the night I drove her home from the restaurant. She'd meant to kiss my cheek, and her tipsy state had her lips landing on the corner of mine. The kiss was over so quickly that it barely registered until the door slammed. Did it scare her that she'd kissed me? Did she expect a bad reaction on my part?

She was perfect, from her curls to the tips of her toes. I wanted her friendship, but I also wanted more. That would take time. She needed to be completely comfortable with me first. The only thing that would make that happen was spending time together. I had plans to have her around a lot in the future.

11

SARI

The house was too quiet. Davina, David's twin, Isa, and Roxie were all stuck at home with kids who'd come down with the flu. The kids who weren't sick had gone to Lanie and Draven's for the night. I'd already made my word count for the day and debated whether to go back to work since Reggie had a better social life than I did. I could call my friends and check in to see what plans they had for the holidays or just catch up on what happened in their lives.

I knew I shouldn't feel bitter that friends I'd had since my mid-twenties or since college weren't ringing me to check how I was settling in or plan a get-together. The abandonment brought up my old insecurities over not fitting in. Yet, I had a good life. I had friends and a very sexy one who was frying whatever brain cells and caution I possessed.

Every time I saw him with Reggie, it made the need worse. He made time for my son, above and beyond what was required as a principal. Reggie loved being able to go to his house to help with the renovations. I knew Reggie had to be more of a hindrance than help sometimes. The man never got frustrated, and Reggie always came home excited to tell me what they'd done—even though Drake sent me a steady stream of pictures. Reggie had come out of his shell so much since we'd moved to town.

Then there was how Drake was with me. His affectionate family could explain all the touches and the way he acted like a gentleman. I started to live for the press of his hand on my lower back. The way he kept me close to his side when we were together. I even liked the way he annoyed me. We'd gone out with Drake to sightsee and check out a few of the unique tourist stops; the antique stores were a favorite as he was looking for period pieces for his house. Reggie and him had finished the second-floor painting and moved to the third level.

I was excited to see the place finished. Yet, because I didn't trust myself, I hadn't gone to his house again. Thanksgiving was coming up, and we'd spend the entire day with him. I'd never done the family thing before. I was still unsure of how easily they accepted me into the fold. Every day I received several texts from each of the Pike family and in-laws. Drake texted me throughout the day to just check on me. Ask about my writing. The ones that made me smile the most were the ones that wanted to know what I was wearing and if I'd send a picture.

He was the biggest flirt I'd ever met, and that said a lot.

I needed something sweet. I gathered the ingredients for a cookies and cream milkshake. With Reggie not there to judge me, I could have what I wanted. That boy of mine thought I ate worse than a kid. I did, but it was easier to grab something simple when I was working.

I dumped everything into the blender, and just as I was about to hit the on button, my phone rang. I answered it without checking the display.

"What are you doing?" Drake asked without a hello.

"Well, I'm making dinner."

"Cookies or ice cream?"

"Um, close, a cookies and cream milkshake." He laughed, and the sound of it warmed me. "What are you doing?"

"Well, I'm bored and thought you'd like to accompany me to the grocery store to get all the stuff for our Thanksgiving and because I know you're going to want to, something to make to take to Mom and Dad's."

"I'm kinda busy, you know, making a milkshake for dinner and watching some mindless comedy. But I think I could keep you company. I could pick up a few things we're low on."

"Don't sound so excited to spend time with me." The pout was clear in his tone.

"How long do I have to get ready?"

"Two minutes, I'm sitting outside your house."

"Confident I didn't have some hot date?"

He snorted. "I would've heard about a hot date. It would've been the latest gossip in the family group text. I'm surprised you haven't been added to it yet. They probably don't want to scare you away with the full extent of the Pike family insanity."

The doorbell rang, and I rolled my eyes as I disconnected the call. I turned on the blender and went to answer the door. When I opened it, he glared at me.

"You hung up on me."

"You were standing outside my door." I turned away and went back to the kitchen, pulling down a tumbler with a lid and straw.

"That's not the point. Phone etiquette, babygirl."

I glanced over my shoulder to see him leaning in the entryway with his arms crossed over his massive chest. I turned back to focus on getting my dinner ready. I turned off the blender, removed the top, and poured the contents into my travel tumbler. I washed everything and put it in the dish drain.

"Give me five minutes to change clothes, and I'll be ready."

"Take your time, Reggie is away, and I'm going to the twenty-four-hour superstore. We're in no hurry."

"Don't touch my milkshake." I pointed at him as I squeezed past to head to my bedroom.

The temperature had dropped, so I picked a baggy turtleneck

sweater to go over my t-shirt, a pair of red pants, and my warmest boots. Once dressed, I adjusted my thick cock because I didn't put on my gaff unless I was wearing a tight dress or skirt. I was too well endowed for it to be comfortable for everyday wear, and my penis never bothered me. I didn't worry with makeup except for some lotion with a bit of tint in it for my face and gloss for my lips. I fluffed my curls until they stood out perfectly and used a tiny amount of hair oil to smooth the frizz that framed my face and bangs. Satisfied I was presentable, I went to rejoin Drake in the kitchen.

"You were eyeing my dinner." I accused, since he was too close to my treat.

"I'm getting you something better than a milkshake for dinner."

"I won't complain about food I don't have to make. With Reggie at your parents, I didn't see the point."

"They were all curled up to watch a movie in the living room with huge bowls of popcorn when I left."

"You stopped by?"

"Yes, I wasn't going to miss out on seeing my second favorite person. He tried to talk me into taking him to my house to do some more painting, but I told him I was going to see if his beautiful mama would spend the evening with me. Tomorrow we'd do some painting."

"Drake, you don't have to let him help. I know he gets more paint on him than your walls."

"He has fun. That's the point. If I have to fix the small section he worked on or wipe drops off the molding, it's not a tragedy. His smile at being helpful and having fun makes it all worthwhile."

I didn't know what to say, so I grabbed my cup and my oversized cotton bag and put my phone inside.

"Did I make you uncomfortable?"

"No, you and your family have been amazing with including

Reggie. I know he still has issues at school, parents who don't invite him to the parties or sleepovers so they don't have to deal with me."

"Hey." He stopped me from turning away by cupping my face in his hands. "He's fine. If those people can't see what an extraordinary kid he is, that's their problem. Me and my family adore him. My nieces and nephews always include him. And if you haven't noticed, my family adores you, too. So, we're going to go have fun because I promised a sweet little boy that his mama wouldn't be lonely." He leaned forward and brushed his lips to my forehead, and then released me.

"I wasn't lonely."

"I was. Saturday is for a boys' night where we do fun things with the kids. I look forward to it. Since you didn't get to go out, I thought you'd enjoy getting out. I know the store isn't exciting, but we're planning our first Thanksgiving, and I want it perfect. I've never made a holiday dinner before. I mean, I've helped, but sharing a dinner with a beautiful woman and her son, that's new."

He turned off lights as he led me to the door with his hand on my back and helped me into my coat that I'd hung on the back of the door with Reggie's school coat and backpack.

"Do you have a list?" I asked as he zipped me up.

"Yes, along with a list of bookmarked recipes. I thought we'd just get a turkey breast since it's just for the three of us, but we can get a small whole one if they have them. I don't think we'll have to fight for whatever's left since we still have a week."

He talked as he locked the door, and we went to his vehicle. As I knew he'd want to, he opened my door, helped me inside, and buckled me in. I didn't want to admit how much I enjoyed these little acts that had become normal for us. My brain was trying to read more into it than there was, but I really liked the sweet man I'd assumed was an asshole when I first met him.

When he backed out of the driveway, he went in the opposite direction of the city. "Where are we going?"

"We're headed south to the twenty-four-hour store off the highway. There are a few places to eat, too. I figured we'd do that before we shopped. I had a sandwich earlier, but it's not holding up."

"Sounds good."

"Did you get in your word count today?"

"Yes. Until you called, I was thinking of putting in a few more hours."

"I'm not messing up your schedule, am I?"

"No, with Reggie away, I didn't have anything else to do. How's the house coming?"

"Good. The biggest thing is finishing the painting. The clawfoot tub I had restored is supposed to be delivered early this coming week. I finished the walk-in shower tile this morning. Other than finding the right furniture for the bedroom and a patio set for the balcony, I think I'm done. David's going to start the landscaping in the spring. He already trimmed the overgrown shrubbery and cleaned out years of weeds."

"Excited to have everything done?" I tucked my left leg under my right and turned slightly to take in his profile. He didn't shave on the weekends, so he was a bit scruffy. His dark brown hair was more silver and gray than brown, but the gray really worked for him.

"Yes. The last few years, I'd started to think it wouldn't get done at all. Something kept coming up, which isn't surprising with how long the house sat neglected. The former owner was elderly, so maintenance wasn't a high priority, and then it sat empty. But I saved a lot by doing most of the work myself and taking advantage of being in a family of contractors."

"You never thought about joining the family business?"

"I'd thought about it, but it wasn't work I loved. It gave me pocket money in high school and helped in college when I moved to off-campus housing."

"Didn't Lanie and Draven help?"

"I didn't want them to. Because I got the scholarship, the money they'd saved for me was divided between my siblings. We were always comfortable, but not rich, and with five kids all wanting to go to college, there wasn't enough otherwise. David and my sisters were the only ones who went. Nolan wanted to work. His college fund was gifted to him when he got married to Roxie to buy a house. They did save some of my college fund. It helped to buy my house. I fought them giving it to me."

"Independent?"

"Not really, but I lucked out. I'd rented a small one-bedroom apartment. I saved and made good investments, so I had a rather good nest egg. Which has a nice dent in it now with the house."

"But are you happy?"

He hesitated, and I frowned. "Yes."

"That wasn't convincing."

"Sorry."

"If you don't want to talk about it, you don't have to."

"It's not that. It's just, I'm going to be fifty beginning of the year. My family worried about me being lonely. And I think I'm lonely sometimes, but I don't know. It's hard to explain."

"You want someone to live in that big house with you."

"I'll admit to that, but I want the right person. I think I've become pickier as I've gotten older. I'm at an age where I want someone. I just don't want the drama that dating brings. I love my life…my family, and I enjoy my job. I don't have anything to complain about. What about you? Are you happy?"

"Very. I have an amazing kid. A successful career that doesn't require me to leave the house and put on grown-up clothes." A rumbling laugh filled the interior. "And lately, I have grown-up conversations. Because of this very nice guy I thought was an asshole, I have a group of friends that I absolutely adore. I have a support system I never had before. I don't have to panic if I have a meeting or with the book tour coming up at the beginning of the year. I don't have to worry about my son being safe and taken care of. I mean, having a partner would be nice. Someone to be there to take the stress off...to tell me I'm not fucking up."

I kept watching him as we made our way to the store. The attractive man was damn near perfect. Someone I would date, but I was too afraid to lose the group of friends I'd made. They were crazy and pushy as hell, but I'd never worried about sending a message to ask for someone to watch Reggie. At almost forty, it was strange. I'd never realized there was a place for me to fit, and it was with a group of people I'd never dreamed of being a part of. Dating never worked out for me, and I didn't know if I was brave enough to take that step.

"If it helps, I don't think you're fucking up."

"It does."

"What do you want for dinner?" he asked and listed the places close to the store.

We chose a place for a quick dinner and spent way too much time shopping. We were both impulsive shoppers, even with a list. I laughed more than I had in years as we fought over things we thought one of us didn't need but ended up throwing them in the cart anyway. Whenever a woman paid him attention and I tried to move away from him, he growled at me and dragged me back to his side.

He made me feel good, and that was dangerous—more than I'd ever dreamed it would be.

12

DRAKE

I was running around my kitchen with my phone tucked between my ear and shoulder as I pulled items from the cabinet and fridge. Sari and Reggie were supposed to be here at any time. I didn't want to look like a moron in front of them or ruin their holiday.

"You're not supposed to cook the stuffing in the turkey, right?" I'd decided to go all out with the full turkey. I hoped I wasn't being too ambitious; I was already scared of screwing up.

"No, it doesn't come up to temp, so you have to mix it and baked it separately. Do you have enough pots and pans for everything?" Mom asked, and I rolled my eyes at her. I could hear the amusement in her voice.

"Yes, I went to the store to buy everything we needed." I didn't want to admit that I'd had the bare minimum in the kitchen because I couldn't be bothered to cook for myself.

"Are you sure you want to make food for them? Maybe impress her some other way."

"I'm not feeling the confidence that I can feed my girl and Reggie. I'm already in a panic over our first holiday together. I need some support, Mom."

I raised my hand to take my phone and leaned back against the counter. The bird was thawed out and ready to go in the oven. I'd pulled the recipes on my tablet, and I'd rested it in a holder.

"Sorry, honey. Don't stress about it too much. Just spend time with them. I'm already sure you've won them over."

"I'm not so sure."

"I've seen the way she looks at you. Maybe she's just unsure of showing her interest. You have all day to feel everything out. When is she showing up?"

"Any time. I told her eleven so we could get started on cooking. She insisted on helping. And the rest of the day I think we're going to relax and watch movies. She said she didn't plan to work at all today. I already made up the guest rooms for them."

"Cooking together is a couple-thing."

"I just want them to have a good day. We'll also be there Sunday."

"Of course you will. That's non-negotiable. Your dad just got home. Have fun and call me later to tell me how everything went."

"I will. Love you."

"I love you, too. And you'll have an amazing day with Sari and Reggie. I don't think you have to work too hard to make them love you."

I thanked her and disconnected the call. I plugged the charger into my phone and put it on silent; I didn't want to be distracted from them; they deserved all my focus to show them they were important to me. Glancing down at myself, I took in my cotton plaid shirt, white v-neck t-shirt, and jeans. I dressed for comfort and told Sari not to worry about getting fancy. We'd be cooking and lounging. Sari said she'd bring Reggie's gaming system to keep him occupied while we cooked.

The floors were chilly under my bare feet, and I wondered if I should start a fire in the living room. Once the cooking started, the kitchen would warm up. All I was going to succeed at was driving myself crazy. The doorbell chimed, and I rushed to the front door, paused, and took deep breaths. As I opened it, a smile tugged at the corners of my mouth.

Sari was standing behind Reggie, he was wearing a jacket, a henley, and jeans, and she was dressed in a long sweater that reached her mid-thighs and leggings. Her hair was a mass of springy curls.

"Come on in." As I stepped back, I pulled the door wider to let them pass.

"We're not too early, are we?" She removed Reggie's jacket, and I took care of hers, and then I hung both and her bag on the coat rack.

"No, perfect timing. I just got off the phone with Mom. Her and Dad were doing lasagna for dinner."

"That sounds good."

"Hopefully not too good. We have a ton of food to make."

"Last year, we had Chinese. And before he came to live with me, I typically worked. So, this is going to be my first official Thanksgiving dinner."

"Reggie, everything is set up for you in the living room to hook up your game or watch TV. Make yourself at home. You already know where everything is." He took off for something more interesting than grownups talking. "Babygirl, you want coffee? I just made a pot."

"That would be great. I was up late to make up for taking a day off. We both slept in, and I only had one cup of coffee."

"That won't do. I also have juice, water, some caffeine-free sodas, and I bought a few bottles of wine."

"Are you ready for this?" she asked as I motioned her forward and followed her.

"You need to sound more confident than me."

"Do we still have time for takeout?" She pivoted on her toes to grin at me as she walked backwards; I loved her bratty expression a little too much.

"No, we're smart, competent adults. We won't be bested by some recipes," I told her, stepping around her when we entered the kitchen. "I figured the turkey's going to take a few hours, at least that's what the package said. While that cooks, we can get the sides prepared. The dressing and mac and cheese will need to go in the oven. Mashed potatoes and veggies won't take long at all. While we're eating dinner, we can throw in the pies you picked. They'll have time to cool for later this evening."

I poured her a cup of coffee and turned around to find her leaned against the island smiling at me. She took the mug with a thanks.

"Sounds like you have a good plan in place."

"I have the recipes and all pulled up on the tablet. Since the turkey takes the longest and it's still early, we have plenty of time. Worst case scenario, we'll have a snack or something."

"Don't worry so much. We don't normally eat until six or seven."

"This is yours and his first Thanksgiving. I want to make sure it's perfect."

I forced myself not to tense as she stepped in front of me and her hands settled on my waist. She was so near all I'd have to do was close the short distance between our mouths. It would be so easy with our heights almost even.

"Nothing is ever perfect, Drake. It's the thought. And if we're eating sandwiches, it's still great."

The sounds of Reggie starting his game carried from the other room, and I instantly felt the loss when she moved away from me. There was no way I was going to resist kissing her before the day was over; I only hoped I didn't make a fool of myself.

"That's him sorted for a while. Check the tablet and make sure

I got everything out. I'll get the turkey in the oven while you start prep on the other stuff."

We stood shoulder to shoulder at the sink to wash our hands, and then we were off in different directions. I told her where to find cutting boards and knives. Prepping the bird seemed easy enough, butter, salt, pepper, and garlic, nothing too difficult or fancy. We worked in silence, and I kept glancing at her as she chopped veggies as I was working at the stove. We moved easily around each other.

"You keep staring. Something on your mind?" she asked as I washed my hands.

"Nothing. Glad you and Reggie could come over today. Much better company than I'm normally used to." I opened the oven and put the roasting pan inside, set the timer, and checked out what we had left to do.

"Didn't want to lay around in your underwear watching TV all day?"

"I can do that any day." She laughed. "What about you? Other than takeout, what did you have planned?"

"Probably put in a few hours working, read while my kid played his game, and then have our takeout. I would've even put it on plates like a respectable mom. So not much different from being here, except for the work and Chinese. I'd still be in my gown."

"Clothes are the bane of adulthood."

"They so are."

I caught her cute pout as she went back to mixing the dressing.

"Sorry."

"It's our lot in life to suffer."

She bumped me with her hip, and then we went back to getting everything ready. What couldn't go in the oven, we stored in the fridge until it was time to put it in the oven. We cleaned up the mess, then put the potatoes on the back burner, ready to start.

I refilled her coffee and led her to the living room, and we took a seat on the couch. She curled her legs to the side. I wanted to pull her close and tuck her to my side, but I didn't know how she'd feel about that; especially in front of Reggie.

While she watched her son play his game, I studied her and the small tilt of her lips.

"You're staring again," she pointed out without looking at me, but I didn't miss the smile that tilted the corner of her plump lips.

"I'm happy you two are spending the day here." I met her gaze as she turned her head, and then I looked at Reggie to find him watching us. I gave him a smile and earned one in return before he went back to playing whatever game. My nieces and nephews didn't play when they came to spend time with me, and when we had family get-togethers, we kept them running so they'd be exhausted at bedtime.

"We're happy to be here, too. I do seem to spend a lot of time at home, so thank you."

"And I told you, you didn't have to say that."

She told Reggie that we'd watch a movie when his character died, and he could play again after dinner. He's replied with a yes, ma'am. Out of all the kids I'd been around, he was the politest I'd ever met. They worked so well as a pair, and I wondered where I'd fit in to that dynamic. There was that insecurity again. I'd never dated a single mother, with my rule of not dating parents of students or any of the teachers. I wondered how they'd make room for me or if they were interested in changing their small family. I could only hope that they had a tiny space available for me.

13

SARI

A s I slowly awakened from a food coma, my first thought
was I would never eat again. The second thought was my
pillow had a heartbeat. I froze as I opened my eyes to find the sun
had set. The TV was on mute. I was sprawled over Drake's big
body, and I panicked as I tried to figure how I'd ended cuddling
up to him. He cupped my ass cheek in one hand, the other curved
around my thigh that laid across his hips, and his face was buried
in my hair.

Shit, how the hell could I get up without waking him? I
shifted, placed my left hand on the couch, and awkwardly tried to
lift my upper body. There was no safe way to move my lower half
without rubbing against a sizable bulge. As I made my first
attempt, he rumbled in his sleep and tightened his hold on me.

"Where you think you're going?"

"You're awake?"

"Yep, and have been for a while. After I tucked Reggie into
bed, I came back down, and you proceeded to use me as a body
pillow."

"Sorry," I apologized as my face heated. "Just let me get up.
You can't be comfortable."

"No need, I'm comfortable."

I lifted my head and rested my chin on his chest. The flickering of the TV illuminated his features. He had that odd half-smile he got sometimes when I caught him looking at me. I held my breath as he swept my bangs to the side.

"Sorry you got stuck with Reggie duty. I should be getting us home."

"Stay. It's late, and he's already in bed. I made up one of the guest rooms for you and already put out a shirt for you to sleep in."

"I don't want to impose."

"You're not. Please stay." I opened my mouth to protest but stopped as he pinched my chin. "Sari, please."

A need filled his eyes that I'd never seen aimed my way before. His gaze dropped to my mouth as his thumb stroked the curve of it. Everything in me froze as I helplessly watched him lift his head. The warm rush of his breath was barely a warning before his lips touched mine. The kiss was soft and gentle, yet also full of heated passion as his hold on my ass tightened, and he urged me higher. His lips were full yet firm.

"Fuck, you're beautiful. Dreamed of this," he whispered before he drew my bottom lip into his mouth, sucking tenderly at it.

As he shifted me to straddle his hips, my heartbeat picked up pace, and blood rushed in my ears. My cock was firming where it pushed to his. What was a teasing exploration turned hotter and fiercer as his grip on my hips tightened with bruising force. As I parted my lips, his tongue met mine and a needy whimper slipped out, mirrored by his gravelly groan. My hips rolled, rubbing our bodies together, and I gasped as his left hand fisted in my curls. He winched my head back, then he licked and bit at my throat.

"That's right, babygirl, just like that." His right hand spread over my ass and tugged me down until there was no space between our lower bodies.

I'd never been this close to getting off so quickly. He bowed his upper body and nuzzled my tiny, unbound breasts through my sweater. I was frustrated by the lack of skin-to-skin contact. He growled a warning deep in his chest as I sat up. I'd worry about consequences later. He wanted me, and I needed to bask in the strangeness of it even for a short time. We'd both come to our senses, but I wanted that memory.

I gripped the hem of my sweater and the camisole beneath, starting to ease them upward, and I stilled. Just as I was about to slip them over my head, rough hands palmed my breasts. Tangled in wool and cotton, a shiver bowed my spine as his lips wrapped around one nipple. The strength of the pull took my breath away, and I was finally able to struggle free of the sweater and tank. My thighs tightened on his waist, and I hugged his head to my chest as he loved on my tiny mounds and pebbled nipples.

His big hands stroked up and down my back. Every time he reached my waist, he jerked my hips closer. The only sounds in the house were moans and groans, harsh, muffled breaths. Sweat broke out on my skin as he loved on me with a passion that bordered on desperation. To be wanted—needed like that, I'd never dreamed. I'd only written about it.

"So soft. So perfect." His reverent tone, the worshipping stroke of his hands and fingertips as they mapped every bare inch of me, it was all too much, but I didn't want to stop. Saying no didn't cross my mind. I needed this too much.

"Mama?" Reggie's voice broke the spell, and Drake pulled me down to hide us with the back of the couch.

"Shit." I whimpered as if the interruption doused me in icy water.

"I got him." His lips brushed mine again, and he groaned as I rolled off him so he could get up.

I laid there on my back, staring up at the ceiling.

"We'll talk when I get back."

That's all he said before I heard him talking to Reggie. I

searched for my discarded sweater, untangled the camisole, and put that back on. What the hell had I done?

"Are you okay?" Drake asked Reggie.

"Yes, I wanted water, but it's too dark."

"I'll get you some nightlights like in your room to put down here. Come on."

I struggled to get my camisole down and then sat up to find them gone. I got off the couch and silently made my way to the kitchen door. I stopped as I heard the fridge door open.

"Where's Mama? Did she leave?"

"No, your mama's just sleeping. She's right there on the couch. Why do you think she'd leave you?" Silence met the question. "Son, a shrug isn't an answer. What's wrong?"

"I dreamed she didn't want me anymore."

I started to rush in at hearing the sadness in my son's voice, but as Drake started talking again, I leaned against the wall to listen. My son liked to make me feel better sometimes, and it should be the other way around. He tried to be brave because he was taught before he came to me that he needed to toughen up. He needed a man-to-man talk with Drake.

"Reggie, there's one thing in this world you can be absolutely sure of. Your mama loves you more than anything. Out of all the babies she could've had, she chose you because in her heart, she knew you were hers. There is no way she'd ever leave you."

My breath hitched as he repeated what I'd told him about adopting Reggie. That was something about him I'd noticed, he listened, and when I or Reggie spoke, he was all in, fully focused.

"Okay."

"Hey, it's okay to feel unsure of things. It's okay to be scared or to cry. You can always go to your mama to talk or me. Feelings aren't bad things. I feel lonely. Even as old as I am, I know I can go to my dad and get a hug or cry on his shoulder. So never be ashamed of just being human, no matter what close-minded people tell you."

"You still cry?"

"Of course, sometimes a really good cry just washes all the stress away."

I eased to the doorway and peeked around the edge to find Reggie seated on the island with a bottle of water hugged to his chest, and Drake had his hands on either side of Reggie's legs.

"A foster father I had told me men don't cry."

"He's wrong and telling you that invalidated the need for men to be emotional. The sooner we teach boys that it's okay to express themselves, the better everything will be. What you learn now will work for you in the future. It will show you how to treat the person you eventually meet."

I smiled as he said person and not girl or woman. It was a shame he didn't have kids of his own; he was loving and compassionate, and unafraid for people to see that.

"Do you want me to get your mama for you?" As he asked, I saw him glance to the door, and he smiled, gave me a wink over Reggie's head. He moved as I entered.

"Hey, baby. Couldn't sleep?" I pretended that I didn't hear; he'd share if he wanted.

"Just wanted some water. Drake got it."

"You want to go home to your own bed?" My son reacted better to being given a choice. I didn't force him into anything except the usual parental rules.

"No, I like it here. Can I take my water upstairs?" He glanced at Drake when he asked.

"You can. I'll make sure you have plenty of light next time you're here."

"Thanks."

Drake lifted Reggie off the counter and put him down. As my son passed me, he gave my legs a hug. "Do you want me to tuck you back in?"

"No, I'm fine."

I watched my tiny, adorable son until he disappeared, and I turned to Drake. "Thank you."

"For what?" He gave me that smile I loved so much.

"For what you said. His psychologist said he's empathetic, but his sensitivity was never validated. As much as I tell him it's okay, maybe he needed a male example."

"I didn't mind. He's so open. Most of the kids I've encountered wouldn't express themselves like him. He's far too mature for his age."

"That's what foster care does for you. It ages you before your time. You become jaded and hardened because everything you know is temporary. You don't find attachments easily. You're just waiting to be tossed aside."

"Come here." He motioned me forward, and I went without hesitation.

I squeaked as he lifted me onto the same spot Reggie had occupied. I was a little taller than Drake. I easily parted my thighs as he moved closer.

"May I take you on a date? A real one. We both get dressed up. Go to a nice restaurant. Play the requisite twenty questions of the first date get to know each other ritual. I want to drop you off afterward and kiss you on your doorstep."

"Why? Why do you want to go out with me?"

"Because I like you. I adore your son. I love you two in my home. You're smart and beautiful, fun, and snarky. I only meant to kiss you but holding you and watching you sleep was amazing. Would it scare you if I said I've never wanted someone as much as I want you?"

I shook my head as he looped his arms around my waist. I felt him lace his fingers at the small of my back. "Are you sure you want to date me? It may cause issues."

"I don't care about the issues. I'll go back to working construction. I enjoy my job, but I don't love it. I loved being a teacher. If you don't want to see where this goes, we can rewind to before the kiss or you removing that sweater."

I tipped my head back at the reminder of what I'd done. I'm not ashamed of my body or that I'm a woman with a cock, it's just what it is, but I've never been the type to rip my clothes off without thinking about the consequences.

"It was very sexy, just so you know." He chuckled. "Look at me, Sari."

I lifted my head to find him studying me. It wasn't an uncomfortable feeling as if he were questioning why he wanted me. He was simply taking me in, and I was still overwhelmed by it.

"I don't just rip my clothes off for people."

"Now I'm feeling special. If you want to try again, I have a nice bedroom with a big bed and a lock on the door." He waggled his brows, and I leaned in, causing his scruff to tease my lips as I brushed my mouth to his.

"I'm not ready for sex, despite my actions earlier."

"You could be completely naked, sprawled in my bed, and no will always mean no. And having you in my bed doesn't mean sex. It means I get to hold you in a more comfortable place than the couch. They were not made for a man my size."

"Or a six-two woman either."

"Have I told you I love how tall you are?"

"Really?"

"You're just my size, and that doesn't happen ever." He answered with his lips against mine.

"I'm taller than you with my stilettos."

"I even love that." I rolled my eyes at his smirk.

"I knew you were weird."

"Halloween almost got you our first kiss."

"Why didn't you then?"

"I don't know? Fear of rejection. I enjoy spending time with you...with the both of you. I didn't want to give that up. But if you want to be friends, we can remain just friends. I want someone who's all in on building a relationship. I'm too old for games and drama. I'm too old to pretend that I don't think this will work. We're already friends. Why not see if we can add another layer."

"I don't want games either. I dated here and there, but I didn't have Reggie then. He's a huge factor in whether it'll work or not. I don't want him to get attached, and then it's suddenly over."

"Why don't we do this...we date but don't tell him yet? We can see where it goes and when the time is right for both of us and we're sure, we let him know."

"You'd do that?"

"Of course. I can tell my parents and siblings to keep their mouths shut when they're watching him for our dates."

"Oh shit, your family. I don't want to lose them either. I love having Mom Friends."

"You won't lose them, I promise. Everyone adores you, and I've remained friends with a few past girlfriends. They even call or text to check-in. So it's not impossible. Don't stress about that. Okay, we go to our separate rooms?"

"For tonight." I tugged at the hem of his t-shirt and twisted my fingers in the soft cotton.

"Perfect."

"I do have a favor?"

"Anything." He couldn't seem to decide between meeting my gaze or let his roam over me.

"Could I get a second t-shirt since I don't have my stuff here? I need to wrap my hair."

"Protect the curls. I'll get you another when we go upstairs."

"Drake?"

"Yes, babygirl?"

"I know I keep saying it, but thanks for all of this. Sharing your family. The time you give Reggie. The space and respect. I really want to see where this goes, but..." I huffed and closed my eyes.

"You don't trust easy. You trust me to keep your son safe and happy. I'll just have to wait a little longer for you to trust me with your safety and happiness. I can be patient. I'm a man who craves taking care of his woman. If it gets too stifling, you can always tell me to back off. Women haven't liked it in the past."

"They didn't like the opening of doors? The demands for text messages? The texts just because throughout the day? I happen to like the gentlemanly Drake Pike. You're a cuddler, so major points there. I've hung out with your family, so I already know everyone is affectionate. Nothing you do will be much of a surprise. You be you. I don't want the person who you think I'd like. That's the only promise I want right now."

"I promise, no hiding myself."

"Good. We better get to bed. The kid will be up at dawn no matter what. He won't come to wake you up, but he'll make enough noise until you do."

"Can I have one more kiss, babygirl?"

I lightly bit my bottom lip as my attention fell to his full, perfectly formed lips. "Please."

His strong hands cupped my jaw. He closed the distance between our mouths, and his nose rubbed the side of mine as he was placing gentle kisses on my lips. He took his time. There was no rush, just tender presses. I moaned as I gripped the sides of his t-shirt. I gasped as he lightly nipped first the top and then bottom.

"One kiss with you is never going to be enough," he gruffly whispered between kisses.

"I'm okay with that." I felt his smile against mine as he suddenly hugged me to his broad chest, my soft stomach conforming to the hard curve of his. I thought he was dangerous when we were just friends. What was going to happen now?

14

DRAKE

Damn, my woman always looked good. She was dressed in a heavy coat and jeans that hugged every inch of her thick legs. She had on a beanie, and her curls framed her beautiful face. Every day that passed, I realized how attached I was to her. It wasn't a simple attraction of needing a gorgeous woman; no, it was everything about her. Her intelligence to her beauty, the way she cared for Reggie.

She was the type of woman, no, she was *the* woman I wanted to build a life with, but I was still a bit insecure about my age. I knew there was only a decade between Sari and I and I shouldn't be hyper fixated on that. Yet here I was. But the connection she and Reggie had didn't seem to leave a lot of room in their small family for me. It was all in my head; yet, it was still there.

I stood off to the side in the shadows, watching her and Reggie walk among the Winter Carnival crowd. It was a huge affair with rides, games, and tons of food. It was a town event, but the businesses and schools took a huge role in organizing everything.

She glanced around as if looking for someone, and I hoped it was me. I weaved through the crowd, and as soon as she spotted me, a bright smile curved her kissable lips. The urge to kiss her hit me, but I refrained. Every time I got her alone, one kiss always led to another. We hadn't repeated what happened on the couch on Thanksgiving. Before the memory of her pretty little nipples on my tongue formed, I brought myself under control.

"Hello, Mr. Pike."

"Hello, Ms. Hampton. You didn't text to say you were on your way."

"You told me you'd be busy. I didn't want to bother you. How's everything going?"

"Good, I can't wait for it to be over."

"Sari, can Reggie walk around with us?"

David's voice drew my attention, and I caught his nod to me, and Reggie barely waited for Sari to give him permission before he was on the move. He made his way through the crowd and then disappeared with my siblings and their kids.

"My kid has a better social life than me."

"Let him have fun and quit pouting. You had to share sooner or later."

"It's still new."

"I got us a babysitter for Friday night."

"You did? And who said I was going out with you Friday?"

"I did."

"Getting all demanding there, Mr. Pike. I may have changed my mind about this."

"No you haven't, and if you didn't freak out, I would've kissed you hello."

As we walked, I brushed my fingers against the side of her thigh, putting my hand on the small of her back to steer us through the crush of people. Even in public, I couldn't keep myself from touching her. I sensed she wasn't ready for me to lace our fingers for anyone to see.

"I wouldn't have complained."

I turned to find her glancing at me. "Don't tease me because I don't care if we're in public. I'd be telling everyone about my woman if you were ready for that."

"Drake."

"Don't say anything. I'm not in this for a few dates. I love spending time with you and Reggie. I'm humbled you let me share him with you." I leaned to the side a bit so no one would hear. "Also, my couch has great memories of you."

She rolled her eyes, but I also caught her grin. I kept reminding myself she needed time, even if I was more than ready to move forward. "I still can't believe I did that."

"Why? A man likes to know his woman wants him so much she loses a bit of control. I haven't done this in a long time."

"Done what?"

At her question and glance, I took her hand and led her into the shadows. I looked around before wrapping her in my arms. "Sari Hampton, you listen, and you listen well. It's been a long time since I wanted someone. I think about you all the time when you're not around, remembering the way you felt in my arms, how those beautiful lips cushion mine just right, or the way you give me that bratty smile when you're giving me shit. Right at this moment, I adore everything about you. I've told you before. I want a date, a hundred dates. I want to spend time just the two of us and also the three of us. If you don't want to see where this relationship that's developing between us goes, then all you have to do is say you want to be just friends. I'll be disappointed, but I respect your decision."

I saw I shocked her, and she just stared at me. I leaned in until the plump curves of her mouth gave so easily under mine as I kissed her how I'd been thinking of since Thanksgiving. Her little moan barely registered in the noise from the crowds, booths, and rides just beyond the darkness where I hid us. I kissed her with all the need I attempted to keep under tight control until she was ready to admit we belonged to each other.

I eased the contact, dropping smaller, quicker kisses on her lips because I was helpless to pull away. I felt the quick rhythm of her breathing where her chest pressed to mine.

"You're too much...sometimes this feels like too much."

"No, you may think that now, but you'll learn that for you...us, we're just right. This is new. We have plenty of time to figure out our way. The way I feel about you is foreign to me...the way I crave you scares me because I don't want to push. Yet, I'm so impatient to have you on my arm for all to see."

"I'll look forward to our date," she whispered, and I stroked her chilled cheeks as she stared at me with an emotion close to awe in her eyes.

"I am, too, now. We're going to walk around until someone needs me for gopher duty. But in the meantime, I'll show off my manly skills of winning my woman something to cuddle with until you let me take over from the stuffed animal."

"Goofy man."

"You like that about me." I smiled as she kissed me again, and I led her back to the crowd.

I didn't want to share her, but I did as I promised and played every game we passed until she had an armful of stuffed animals that she handed out to kids without one. Except for one, a fluffy teddy bear with a bowtie that she hugged to her chest.

"Not going to give away another one of my hard-earned gifts?"

"No, this is my Drake Bear, and he has a very important job for a while. Maybe a long, long, long while."

"Better not be a long while."

She snorted at me. "You're too easy to tease, and I thought you were patient."

"About some things. And while I'll suffer until you put me out of my misery, don't tease. It's mean, babygirl."

"I'm sorry. I won't be mean."

I squeezed her fingers that were teasing my palm, and I barely resisted lacing our fingers.

"Mr. Pike." I groaned, hearing my name yelled.

"I'll find you as soon as I'm done with whatever they want, or do you want to come with me?"

"No, you go do what you need to. I'm going to hunt down your family and my kid to see what trouble he's getting into."

"Have fun. Text me when you find them."

She nodded, and I took off to see what they needed. I couldn't wait for our date so we could spend time together without interruptions, but if everyone knew we were dating, I could drag her along with me. I shouldn't be this obsessed with a woman I'd only known a matter of months, but the moment I'd seen her crouched down in front of her son, I knew there was something special about the gorgeous woman.

The more time we spent together, the more the intensity of the attraction became. Even the one woman I'd thought about asking to marry me hadn't brought out this level of need and possessiveness. I should temper it, but I couldn't. I didn't want to be anyone other than myself with Sari; to let her know how I felt and that she could trust me.

My woman was perfect in every way, and I enjoyed the hum of arousal that hit me just being in her presence or when I thought about her. I'd never felt like this before, it intoxicated me, and I may be more than a little addicted to the newness. But for me, I sensed that it would always be that way between us. In my gut and heart, I knew she was the one I'd waited for.

15

SARI

I couldn't remember the last time someone picked me up for a date. Normally, we'd pick a meet-up point and go from there, but I stood in front of my mirror to check my reflection. My curls were perfect. My skin moisturized and glowing under the bright overhead light. I'd gone with a pretty, yellow sweater dress that clung to my thick curves, and I zipped up a pair of matching stiletto boots. My black trench coat would go over it.

Draven had already picked up Reggie to take him home for the weekend. He'd be camping the next night with Drake and the guys, and I'd get him back during the usual Sunday dinner. When I'd moved here, I'd had my doubts about the small community. Everyone was nice and laidback, although there were a few assholes about, but that happened everywhere.

I smoothed the sweater dress over my hips and then picked up my black clutch purse that was big enough for lipstick, phone, cards, and wallet. I second-guessed my choice of shoes, but it's not like Drake didn't know my height, and he said he loved I was taller than him in my heels. We had to be a sight, him at six and a half feet and me only a little shorter than him in flats. Even in my heels, I still felt almost delicate beside him, as if I physically fit with someone for the first time in my life.

He even said he'd wanted to kiss me at the start of the Winter Carnival for everyone to see. A part of me always waited for the newness to wear off, especially after we'd gotten caught up in the moment on Thanksgiving. While I wasn't typically a self-conscious woman, knowing I was Trans and feeling the proof were two different things. I'd had a few sexual experiences that hadn't gone well.

I shook off the train of thought. I wasn't going to question us. He wanted to take me on a date. In some ways, I think he might want more, and my body was ready, but my mind and heart were telling me to be cautious.

The peal of the doorbell had me rushing for the door with my coat and purse. When I opened it, I froze at the sight of Drake in a tailored suit that highlighted the width of his shoulders and chest. I'd appreciated how a man looked in a suit before, but something about Drake looking all elegant in the dove gray three-piece suit was almost obscene.

"Wow, you look even more gorgeous than normal." He stepped inside, his left arm going around my waist as he tipped his chin to give me a soft hello kiss.

"And you know you're gorgeous."

"Thank you. I changed suits four times."

"Why?"

His hand spread across my lower back. "Because I'm desperate for this date to go well so you'll want to do it again."

"That's cute."

"I'm supposed to be sexy, baby, not cute."

I stroked my fingertips down his striped tie. "You're sexy, too. But it's also cute that you want to make sure I enjoy our date. But I want you to like it, too."

"And I will since I'll be spending it with you. To me, this is just the first date of many. I'm going to be calling in a lot of IOUs for my past babysitting."

"We haven't even been out yet, and I approve your plan."

He helped me on with my coat and then turned me to face him as he did up the buttons and tied the belt. All I could do was stare as he fussed over me until he was convinced that I was warm enough. And as he always did, when he led me outside, he opened my door and buckled me in. I loved his gentlemanly ways and how natural it came to him. His brothers, brothers-in-law, and dad were the same. In the time I'd come to know them, I'd learned Draven had set an example for his sons on how to treat their person and taught his daughters what they should demand from their partners.

"What has you such deep in thought?"

"It's nothing bad. I told you about being in foster care. There were good homes, but for the most part, a lot of kids are just checks every month. I was thinking about your dad."

"What about Dad?" he asked as he backed out of the driveaway and onto the street.

"Well, about your mom, too, But mostly your dad. He taught you and your siblings about how to treat and be treated. Your sisters found men very much like y'all. Gentlemen. Your dad showed by example. When you're a gentleman, I can see how it's ingrained. I don't think you're even conscious that you do it."

"Oh, I'm conscious of it, but it's natural. Dad always said in order to keep your person happy...you need to show them their importance to you in the way you treat them. My grandfather was a cold, hard man. Dad said he couldn't remember him saying I love you, or he was proud at any point in his life. It's imperative that you let the person you're with and your children know how you feel. It creates an emotional security and safety. Yet, anyone can say the words, but if we can't back it up in our care and affection, then it's all very much pointless."

"So, it's more about caring than love?" I turned to watch him as we passed under the streetlights. He occasionally turned to glance at me with that open smile of his. I loved he wasn't one to hide his emotions.

"Both are important. Like I said, anyone can romantically say I love you for hundreds of superficial reasons, but if there's nothing behind them, what's the point? It's essential to remember the little things. Something they mentioned they liked or a milestone anniversary. It's little touches just because. Pulling them closer at night when they move away in their sleep."

"Why the hell are you single?"

"My parents. My mother is a strong, independent woman, but she allows Dad to take care of her. And I asked him once what was the key to them staying together so long."

"And what did he say?"

"Her smile. Because he knew he'd put it there and never gave her reason to lose it, and if she ever did, he made sure it always came back."

Everything in me went still at his explanation. I'd heard a lot of advice. I wrote romance for a damn living, and I'd never heard it explained so simply and beautifully in my life. At forty, I'd never once felt that sense of peace and wonder being with a person, friend, or partner.

"You're awful quiet."

"At my age, I've never come close to anything remotely like your parents' or siblings' marriages. I've felt envy and loneliness, asked myself why it never worked out before, but I never realized it could be so simple yet profound."

"It's not simple. They've fought like hell. Yet even in their anger and hurt, they knew they were made for each other. They never went to bed angry, even if that meant a sleepless night or two. It's rare to find a bond like that, and I'm jealous as hell."

I was about to answer, but he turned on the signal and pulled into the parking lot of a small building. Electric candles burned in the windows on either side of the front door.

"I hope you like this place. This is the usual date night restaurant for the family."

"I'm sure it's great."

"I'll come around and get you."

I hid my smile as he got out, and I watched him circle the front of his vehicle until he opened my door. He unbuckled my seatbelt and offered me his hand. It was easy to slide out because of my height, but I loved being his focus. I saw it with Reggie, too. When Reggie spoke or wanted to show him something, Drake put him first. He was too easily knocking down all the walls I'd erected in my life to keep myself safe.

He laced his fingers through mine after locking the SUV, and we walked across the lot. Once inside, we were quickly led to a table, asked what we wanted to drink, and were left with menus.

"How's your deadline coming along?"

"It's good. Hit a wall a few days ago and had to go back to move some things around. I sent the rewritten chapters off to Janice, and she seemed pleased."

"What about you?"

"A lot of Creatives spend their time mired in the quicksand of imposter syndrome. Also, I hadn't planned on writing romance. Although, from what I hear and see of my reviews, I don't do too badly of a job."

"I'm sure you're excellent. The ladies brag on you all the time."

"That's nice of them. I spent most of my career writing nonfiction. Even put my nose in business a few times I was told I should stay away from."

"Do you miss the excitement?"

"Sometimes. But having Reggie is more important than chasing the adrenaline high of a dangerous story. What about you? You said you missed teaching."

The server arrived with their wine, and he thanked her, then took a sip as we let her know we weren't ready to order yet. I wasn't in any hurry to rush our night ahead.

"I do miss the teaching, but I had the qualifications, and they desperately needed a principal. I took it. It's not all bad. I'm just not one for the politics involved. And it's year-round, so I miss those summer vacations. Look at the menu. I need to get you fed."

We talked about anything and everything, silliness to politics. It was the best date I'd ever had. It was fun and comfortable, and I didn't once notice anyone staring or pointing at us. Like him, I wanted more dates, times where we shared dinner out or meals at home with Reggie. I wanted it all, and I didn't quite know how to accept and trust our relationship. My uneasiness wasn't about Drake; it was if I could let go of years of building my walls and tear them down for him. I glanced up from my plate when fingertips stroke the back of my hand.

"No heavy thoughts, just be here with me, nowhere else, Sari."

I laced our fingertips as I gave him a smile. He made everything okay just by being, but could I do the same for him?

16

DRAKE

She giggled as I nuzzled the side of her neck as she tried to make us dinner. She had on one of her cotton turbans, giving me perfect access to her throat. We'd enjoyed our first and second date, and the third was at my place. With the Winter Carnival over, it was the toy drive and Christmas Break coming up, so we'd missed spending time together. The kids were spending the night at Davina and Tolliver's house, so I'd brought Sari home with me.

It hadn't missed my attention that she craved my touch and presence when we were close. I was addicted to the feel of her tall, soft body against mine. She gasped as I nipped her earlobe and eased my hands under her t-shirt. Her stomach gave under the pressure of my hands, dragging them up until my fingertips met the lower curve of her breasts. And then I went higher until the curves fit just in the cups of my palms.

"Turn the stove off." I heard the click and the pan sliding off one of the front grates to a back one. I hugged her and lifted her feet off the ground.

I ignored her telling me to put her down because she was too heavy, and I made my way to the nearest soft surface—the couch.

I placed her back on her feet. The lamps dimly lit the room, but I'd want full light soon. Right that minute, all I wanted to do was learn what she liked. When I spun her to face me, I tugged her closer with my hands on her hips. Her firm ridge behind her zipper lined up perfectly with mine. I wanted her naked so badly.

Falling backward, I took her with me, and when we landed, she was straddling my thighs. Behind the desire I saw on her face, I also saw concern and a bit of fear.

"Why are you scared?"

"I don't know. I feel safe with you, but…I haven't done this in a long time."

"Me either. I had an embarrassing one-night-stand attempt a year ago."

"Embarrassing?"

I didn't want to tell the story, but I needed her to know that I didn't take what we were doing lightly. Just looking at her turned me on, and that had never happened. I felt as if I desired her too much. "I'd never done one before, it's not my thing, and it was so awkward. But I was out of town, and I had a few too many. Let's just say nothing worked."

"I don't think you have that problem right now." She rolled her hips, and I groaned.

"No, no problem." My voice broke as she did it again, and I grabbed her hips in a hard grip.

"Too much there?" I stretched up to kiss her sexy smirk.

"I don't want to embarrass myself with you."

"What grown-ass woman doesn't want to know her man is so on edge, her touch makes him lose control?"

I shivered as she moved her hands under my t-shirt to stroke over the hairy curve of my belly. She hummed her approval.

"Did I tell you that I fantasized about how hairy you are?" I shook my head, and my hips jerked as she tugged the hair on my chest. I straightened and practically ripped the shirt over my head.

"I want to feel your skin on mine. Take this off." I tugged at the bottom of her t-shirt, and she didn't hesitate to give me what I wanted. Her smooth, soft brown skin had a smattering of freckles. They were on her nose and cheeks as well. When her upper body was bare, she rested her chest to mine, and I captured her mouth.

All our control slipped as we kissed and touched. We shared groans and whimpers as she sensuously rubbed her breasts through the thick brown hair on my chest that was liberally streaked with silver. We only separated when we needed to catch our breath, but it didn't last long. I pushed my fingers under the waistband of her jeans to cup the plump curves of her ass cheeks. I squeezed, loving the way they overflowed my hands. There was something about small breasts and a big ass that just did it for me.

My cock was painfully trapped in my jeans, but this wasn't about me. I wanted to see my gorgeous woman get off. I reluctantly pulled my hands from beneath the denim and stroked them around to the button. I trapped her bottom lip between my teeth. I slowly released it as I took in her heavy-lidded eyes. Her sweaty skin was slick against mine. If it was this good just making out, what happened when I got her in my bed?

"May I?" She nodded, and that wasn't good enough. "No, I want the words, babygirl."

"Do I have to do it myself?"

"I love when you get snarky." I grinned as I popped the button on her jeans, carefully easing the zipper down. "What do you like?" I asked as she whined while I pulled her from her jeans and stroked the firm length. She was completely waxed at the base, her sac smooth and soft.

"I don't stay hard. It's frustrating if I lose it. It has nothing to do with whether I want you or not, but I usually take something when I top."

"Is that what you like?"

"I..." Her nails dug into my chest as I jacked her in a slow, teasing rhythm. "I'm versatile, but my preference is to bottom." She pressed her mouth to mine. "You going to show me what you got for me?"

"Yes, but I want to see all of you."

I felt her loss as she eased off my lap and stood in the small space between the coffee table and the couch. My hands shook as I unbuttoned my pants and eased the zipper down. I hooked my thumbs in the waist of my jeans and briefs. I couldn't take my focus from her as she removed her turban first and let her curls free. And then she removed her pants and panties.

Her length was heavy between her thighs. She was flawless dark skin over thick, supple curves.

"Did you forget something?" she asked as she shook out her hair.

It took me a minute to realize I'd stopped with the fabric wrapped around my thighs. She turned away, and I groaned as she bent at the waist to move the table away. I roughly shoved my clothes down and tossed them to join hers. Before she could straighten, I grabbed her hips and pulled until she landed on my lap. My dick notched perfectly between her ass cheeks. My left hand curled around the front of her throat and brought her head back to rest on my shoulder. My right wrapped around her cock.

"Drake," she whispered as she leaned slightly to the side and turned her head until her lips brushed against mine. As she rode my thick cock, precum started to ease the slide, and I realized we were both panting. I protested as she removed my hand from her length, and she brought it to her mouth. "I need a little more lubrication."

She nipped at my fingertips, and my left hand tightened around her throat as she sucked two of my fingers past her plump lips. Lust seized my muscles and cleared my brain. All I could focus on was her sucking my fingers, her lush ass working my cock, and I was too on edge. I moaned as she released the middle and index fingers. She nipped at the base of my thumb and licked a slow path across my palm.

My mouth slammed against hers as she curled my hand around her cock. My tongue teased hers, and I matched my strokes to the quickening pace of her hips. She lifted her right arm, and her hand fisted in my hair. Our kiss ended, but she didn't take her lips from mine. Rumbles and high-pitched, sharp moans met as our sweaty bodies worked for release. The sting of her pulling my hair, and hers teasing my shoulder. Her nails pushed into the arm that was jacking her.

"Fuck, babygirl, you gotta give it to me." I pressed my forehead to hers. "Too close." My balls drew up and ached, and my upward hip movements that met the downward roll of hers stuttered.

"No, you give it to me, Daddy." No woman had ever called me Daddy and her husky, pleasure tortured tone saying it threatened to break me, but I refused to do anything to hurt her. "Take it. Lose control. I won't break."

My arm was a band around her stomach as I forced her to still. I bit and sucked at her shoulder as I tightened my grip on her cock. She was bucking and fighting my hold, a scream tore from her throat, and her body bowed forward. She jerked her thighs wider and lifted, and I gritted my teeth and begged my body to hold off.

As she came, she abruptly collapsed onto my chest, and I worked the swollen head of her cock until she pushed my hand away.

"Suck me." I didn't recognize my own voice, and for a second, I thought I went too far until she was off my lap and on her knees between my legs. "Fuck." I shouted as she barely lifted my dick from my belly before she swallowed me to the back of her throat.

My fingers tangled in her curls as my body took over, and I thrust up as she sucked me. My ass muscles flexed and my thighs strained, and all I could do was watch as my thick girth disappeared and appeared between her swollen lips. She was humming and moaning, and then I noticed the movements of her body. She was stroking herself as she sucked my dick.

I did that to her. I turned her on so much that giving me head gave her pleasure. I froze on an upward roll of my hips, and I pulled her head down until her nose was buried in my pubes. I shot down her throat, and each contraction of her throat as she swallowed made me get off harder. My chest heaved as I relaxed boneless to the couch, and I watched her from under my lashes as she licked me clean with a smile on her face.

"Get your ass up here." My deep voice was barely more than a growl as she crawled up into my lap. I violently brought her mouth to mine and thrust my tongue past her lips, tasting myself. I gentled the kiss, then cleaned her lips of the release that she hadn't been able to swallow. "I should've asked if you were okay with that."

"If I minded, you would've known about it." She cuddled to my chest and tucked her face against my neck as I drew my fingertips along the indent of her spine. I felt the swipe of her tongue across my skin and then a sharp nip. "Seems Daddy is a trigger word."

"No woman has ever called me that before. I didn't know it was."

As much as I enjoyed having sex with her the first time, the cuddling and gentling afterward were just what I needed, too. Women didn't normally let me have this.

"What are you thinking about? Doubts?"

"No, I missed this."

"The sex or the cuddling."

"Both."

"What did your other women do? Get up and go home?"

"Pretty much. The last one was two years ago. She got up, showered, and said she had an early morning."

"She totally missed out. My past relationships were extremely short, and they didn't stick around afterward either. Except for the polite post-coital embrace before they pissed and ran out the door. I sleep on the left side of the bed. I do not compromise, but I need water and a shower before bed."

"Does that mean I get to keep you all night?"

"Yes, but you also have to feed me. My snack was high in protein but calorie-wise, not so much."

I snorted embarrassingly loud, and she chuckled as she hugged my waist. "Get up, we'll take a shower, and then I'll see if I can salvage our dinner that I probably ruined."

"It wasn't ruined. I've done a lot of things I regret in my forty years, but this definitely isn't one of them." She lifted her head to smile at me.

"I have no doubts or regrets. This…what we're working on… is just what I want. We can still go as slow as you want."

"I think third date was pretty slow, but if we factor in family time as dates, we've been taking it as a snail's pace."

"I like the way you think."

"Of course you do. I just fried your brain cells with an epic blowjob."

I tipped my head back as if I were thinking, and I hissed as she straightened and pulled my chest hair. "Hey, you like that hair don't rip a bald spot."

"Think about that next time you want to act a fool."

"Hunger is making you cranky. Let's get a shower." I kissed her gently before I helped her off my lap, and I eased off the couch. "Go on upstairs. I'll be right behind you." I bent to pick up our discarded clothes and quickly caught up to her taking the steps. I took in the sway of her hips and the bounce of her ass.

She was mine, and I'd never take that for granted; I just had to get her to fall as hard for me as I had for her. Everything would be perfect then.

17

SARI

"Come on, Daddy, you ain't coming out to say hi to me?" I kept my voice low as Drake growled in my ear; I'd become addicted to frustrating him. I showed up early to pick up Reggie and leaned back against the grille of my SUV in perfect line of sight to Drake's office.

"I can see you just fine from here."

I sneakily stroked my tongue over my lower lip, and I laughed as I heard him curse. A voice I recognized as the office receptionist asked was everything okay. Days passed since we'd spent time alone. When he'd said that he'd take it slow and follow my lead, he wasn't lying to me.

"Yes, yes, I'm fine. I just dropped my coffee mug." It got quiet. "You're having way too much fun at my expense."

"You do tend to have a little problem when I'm around. I'm drunk with all this power."

"You two coming to spend the weekend with me?"

"What about ladies' night? I couldn't miss that."

"Forget ladies' night. We can take Reggie to do something fun all day, tire him out, and then you and me, alone time. What sounds better, getting drunk with the ladies or spending the night with me?"

"Well, that's kind of a hard decision. I mean, I could go out and have fun with your sisters and sisters-in-law, or I could hang out in your old, drafty house?"

"You know I can keep you warm."

"It is like having my own furry, electric blanket. No time for us the rest of the week?"

"Committee meetings, the last push at the toy drive and donations, and we have one more week before Christmas break. We need to go shopping."

"I don't know who you're talking to. All my shopping was done a week ago."

"Now you're making me feel like a slacker. You have to send me Reggie's list of what you got him so I don't get the same things, and I also need your list of what you want."

"You know what I want," I said as the buses started pulling up in front of the school and blocked my view of the office. I tried to warn myself that I didn't want to get in over my head too quickly. Unfortunately, my son and I were already attached.

"This weekend is all yours, I promise. Soon, this holiday mess will be over with."

"I know. I just like giving you a hard time in more ways than one."

"You really do, babygirl. Okay, that's the bell. I have to supervise."

"Are you wearing your gray suit today? Because I have to say, Mr. Pike, you're exceptionally sexy in that one."

"Sari."

"Yeah, yeah, ruin my fun, Daddy. Act all respectable. Call me when you get home?"

"Of course."

We said goodbye, and I disconnected my call, slipping my phone into the pocket of my skirt. I crossed the drive, slipping between the buses, and stepped up onto the curb. I smiled as my son exited with Drake close behind him. The day was chilly but not too bad, but I'd bundled Reggie up that morning. My son wrapped himself around my legs as I caught Drake's gaze with mine. The breeze ruffled his silver and brown hair, and he gave me a wink.

"How was your day, love?" I asked as I took Reggie's hand and led him back to the car.

"It was okay. Are we going to Drake's tonight?"

"No, this weekend." His disappointment hit me hard, but I sympathized because keeping a discreet distance grew harder after our weekend. I opened the door and stood back as he climbed in. He was getting more independent since we moved, especially with spending time with Drake and his family. "What do you want to do tonight?"

"Grilled cheese and a movie?"

He let out a disgusted huff as I paused to think about it. "I guess I can do that. Flipping that heavy sandwich, I'm going to be so exhausted."

"Drake would make it for me."

I rolled my lips between my teeth to hide my smile. He was playing the *Drake Card*, just what I needed; the two men in my life ganging up on me. I buckled him in and closed the door. I don't know if he saw Drake as a father figure or viewed him as more like an uncle. As much as I wanted to ask what he thought about Drake, we still hadn't discussed what was really going on. We needed to have a talk about Reggie and if we should talk to him.

I felt myself holding back, and I didn't know why. What would be so wrong with being official? It wasn't like I was in my twenties and still didn't know what I wanted from my life. I put on my seatbelt, turned on the engine, and backed out to make the slow progress out of the parking lot.

"Mama?"

"Yeah, love?"

"What are we doing for Christmas? Are we going to go to grandma and grandpa's?"

"We're going Christmas Eve, and we're going to Drake's Christmas Day." I glanced in the rearview and noticed him worrying his bottom lip between his teeth. "Something on your mind?"

"I have to get Drake a present."

"What about when I pick you up from school Friday, we go find him something."

"Really?"

"Of course, love. Why don't you think about what you want to get him before then, okay?"

He nodded as I turned onto our street. I knew my son would worry himself crazy by the time Friday came around, but I knew it was important to him. As soon as I parked, Reggie was out of his seat and rushed to the door to unlock it.

"You're such a gentleman, love," I hollered as I got out, and he disappeared inside. We really needed to work on his manners a bit. I stretched across the seat to get my bag from the passenger side and went to get my son his snack.

My son's need for routine had lessened some. It was more habit than anything. As I removed my coat, I noticed his backpack and jacket in the middle of the floor. "Reginald Harvey Hampton, pick up your bag and get me your folder."

His little feet pounded on the hardwood floor as he snatched up his bag and hung it and his jacket on the hook. He dug out his folder and took off for the kitchen. I bent over to remove my fleece-lined boots, and I placed them next to Reggie's boots, then made my way to the kitchen. I took a seat at the table as I picked up his folder and went through it, looking for homework or anything that needed a signature.

Reggie searched for a snack.

"Love, come here a minute?" I pushed out the chair beside me with my toes and waited for him to sit down. "I wanted to talk to you about something."

"Am I in trouble?"

"Of course not, but I wanted to ask you about something important."

"Okay."

"What do you think about if your mama wanted to date someone?"

"Would they like me?" I stretched out my arm and rubbed his cheek, and then I let it fall to the table.

"They would have to like you, love, and you'd have to like them. You know I'll love you no different if I met someone, you know that, right?"

"Yes, Mama. Would it be a boy or a girl?"

"I don't know. You know I just want a person. Their gender isn't important to me. But you've been with me for two years now. This was something we'd never discussed. So if your old mama met someone, it would be okay with you?"

"As long as they like me, too. Can I have my snack?"

"You can. While you have that, I'm going to go check my email. Think about what movie you want to watch, and I'll make grilled cheese and soup for dinner."

He nodded and jumped down from his chair. That was easy enough, but I knew it would be different when I introduced him to someone. Yet he wouldn't mind if my person was Drake. I pushed up from the chair and walked to my office. I plopped into my desk chair, but I didn't wake up my laptop. Janice was due to send me an email with a tour schedule, and edits were due with a cover mock-up. I hadn't grown comfortable with the thought of being on display. Compliments and social interactions weren't my things so that's why I'd avoided this as long as possible.

It was easier when I was a journalist. My name was in the byline and nothing else. The idea of being an author was never on my to-do list, well, maybe nonfiction, but the romance went too well. I wouldn't complain because it gave me the chance to spend as much time with my boy as I wanted.

I was a mother as I always wanted to be. It was time that I seriously considered adding to the family. I liked Drake, and I could see myself falling for him if I hadn't already. He treated me with respect—he was gentlemanly, smart, and handsome, and he was everything a woman would want. So why was I so scared to make it official? He wouldn't reject me. He was only waiting for me to decide.

All I needed to do was open my mouth and say I wanted to take our relationship public, but I needed to discuss if Drake was ready for a ready-made family. If he wasn't ready to be a dad, maybe it was best to go back to friends.

18

DRAKE

I stood in the doorway of the guest room to watch Sari cuddling Reggie. She was scratching his head as he dozed off. He had started running a fever the previous night when we'd returned from my parents' place. With him not feeling well, I told Sari to spend the night at my home so she didn't have to bring him out. She'd left to grab all the presents so he could open them there.

Our time together reached the bare minimum, but with holidays almost done, I was going to focus all my attention on them. She'd been quiet the past few weeks, and I worried about what was wrong. As much as she said nothing, we needed time to talk. I talked to my parents about how I wanted to take my and Sari's relationship to the next level.

They mentioned her caution might be due to not wanting to hurt Reggie. I'd thought I'd made it clear that I was all in. I smiled as she glanced at me as she started to ease off the bed before tightly tucking the covers around his tiny body. She leaned over and brushed her lips to his forehead. I backed into the hall as she turned off the bedside lamp and the nightlights turned on.

I'd placed them all over the house so that he could always find his way. She left the door ajar and turned to me.

"Is he okay?"

"His fever is down. I think he'll be back to his old self tomorrow."

"Come on downstairs. I'll get you some tea." I laced my fingers through hers and brought her hand up to press a kiss to her knuckles.

As I walked with her to the first floor, unwrapped presents surrounded the tree I'd bought just for Reggie. I wanted to show her that he was as important to me as she was. I released her hand to fill up the electric kettle and then grabbed two mugs. Glancing over my shoulder, I found her staring at me.

"You've been quiet lately. Something wrong?"

"No, nothing wrong. Where do you see this relationship going?"

"You want to know my intentions?"

She shrugged. "I've never been in this position before. I mean, I told you I'd dated in the past, but everything's different now that I have to think about someone other than myself. Reggie likes you. He's attached, and I don't want him hurt if this implodes."

I turned around to face her, our bodies separated by only a few feet as she mirrored my position where she was leaning against the island. In the time we were apart, I'd done research on sex to make it good for her if she ever wanted to go there. I'd never prioritized the act of sex. I loved the other stuff, and I learned that some Trans women required more foreplay, and I had no problems with that. Yet since our night together, we hadn't really done more than flirt.

"If you want to know my intentions, I'd like for this to be outside your house or mine. I want to be able to hold your hand in public. Take you on a date and not pretend that it's just two friends out. But there's more than you and me involved in this decision." She nodded, and I continued. "Reggie is as important to me as you are. I understand we need to take it slow for his sake. I don't see what we have imploding. Things have been crazy, and I know I haven't spent enough time with you and him."

"You know I'm out. I won't go back into the closet. My life is very much in the open."

"And I have no problem with that. I thought I'd made that clear. I adore you, Sari. I look forward to the time I get to spend with you two and also our one-on-one time. I want to make a go of this relationship. But I'm just me trying to find my place in your family. So if you want to keep everyone thinking we're friends, then that's what we'll do, but that isn't what I want."

"I don't want that either. I asked Reggie what he'd think of me dating. All he wanted to know was would the person like him. He knows that his mama could bring home a boyfriend or a girlfriend. He knows his mama is a Trans woman. I'm always honest with him…knowledge to me is power. So keeping this secret from him doesn't sit right with me."

"Then do you want to take our relationship public? Tell everyone we're exclusive? We can date, see if we can make this work. I'm sure we can." I closed the distance between us and brought my hands forward to rest on her sides just above the flare of her hips.

"I guess it's all official then." She tipped her chin, and I brought my mouth down on hers.

I planned just one kiss, but with her, one never satisfied me. My need for her took over, we were never close enough, and the weeks of restraint broke me. She wrapped her arms around my neck as her lush lips parted. Kissing and holding her reached the top of my favorite things. I felt so out of my element with her.

"This shouldn't be there when you're kissing me." She stroked the furrows between my brows. I closed my eyes as the back of her fingers caressed my cheeks.

"I feel like I don't know what the hell I'm doing."

"Why? Explain it to me."

"Before you, I didn't really think about a physical relationship. I love the dating and then the intimacy of being with someone. Sexually, I could take it or leave it. With you, I don't know, kissing and touching you...there's never enough."

"You know, there's a word for that. Let me ask you, does sex only happen after you've developed an emotional attachment to someone?"

"Yeah, but it's different with you. Just hearing your voice makes me want you."

"You could be on the asexual spectrum. Demisexuals don't feel a sexual attraction to someone until they've connected emotionally to that person."

"Really?" She nodded and smiled at me. I hated to admit I never studied the facets of the LGBTQ community. Who someone dates or loves isn't my place to judge. To me, if someone made another person happy, why not celebrate someone finding their person.

"I have friends who are sex-indifferent or sex-repulsed. They have no interest in sexual relationships at all. I have some friends who like intimacy but no penetration or need for an orgasm. I'm a Trans woman who has topped my male and female partners. My penis makes me no less a woman. What I enjoy in bed doesn't change who I am. Sex and gender are for a person to define for themselves. I can't say if you're demi, that's for you to figure out on your own. But if it eases your worry, I love how affectionate you are with me. You can kiss and touch me as much as you want, and I won't complain because I like being with you."

"And I love you being here. I know our pasts are different. I understand the fact I have to earn your and Reggie's trust, and having that humbles me. It's not easy for you two to let someone else in. That's why I don't want to rush." I nudged her nose with mine and brushed my mouth to hers. "I want this. I want you. I'll never hurt either of you intentionally. I can't make promises that I'm not sure I can keep."

"I know, and that's why I let my guard down with you. Reggie liking you is a major point in your favor. Before I fostered and adopted him, dating was a non-issue. If I got hurt, I'm a big girl, I can take it. He's already looking at you as a role model. He calls your parents grandma and grandpa. He's entered your family unit and found his place. I can't take that away from him. My son is finding everything he never believed in, and I need him to believe in the good…that family stays."

"They love Reggie. It would devastate them to lose him."

"Did I ever tell you that I've rarely met a man who isn't afraid to voice his feelings…his concerns? Society teaches boys that emotions are bad. You have grown men saying *No Homo* when they do something that may be considered non-masculine. There's not an ounce of toxic masculinity in this big body of yours. And that makes you sexier. You weren't taught the bad things about gender and roles."

"You know what they say. All the ladies want the bad boys, though."

"Nope, not my thing. Big, handsome, gentlemanly men are my type, Daddy." She nipped at my chin and used her nose to nudge my head back. She bit and sucked lightly at my throat; I pulled her flush against me. "So responsive." She nuzzled my chest hair exposed by my gray tank.

My hips humped into her hand that palmed my quickly hardening dick. The only thing between her touch and my cock was my baggy workout shorts.

"Is this all for me, Daddy?"

"Yes." I hissed the answer as her fingertips lightly stroked the tip. I knew she'd feel the wet spot of precum that was quickly spreading. "Babygirl, you're going to make me go off."

She lifted onto her tiptoes and urged my mouth to hers. As she sucked my bottom lip into her mouth, she eased her hand into my shorts. She cupped my balls, and her nails tickled my taint.

"Fuck."

"Not yet. Your babygirl isn't ready, but that doesn't mean I can't get Daddy off." She spun me until I took her place against the island. She dropped to her knees and pulled my shorts down to the middle of my thighs. My cock stood out hard, the tip beaded with precum. Her pink tongue peeked from between her lips, and I gripped the counter as she tongued my slit. Her dark, beautiful eyes focused on my face.

I swallowed a loud groan as she wrapped those perfect lips around the fat head and sucked me to the back of her throat. My girth stretched her lips wide. I threw my head back as her hands slipped under my shirt. She tugged the hair as she slowly worked her way up to my nipples. As soon as she scratched over them, my hips thrust forward. I panicked that I may have hurt her, and I lifted my head to take in the sight of her there.

Her curls framed her beautiful face. She bobbed along my length like she'd never had anything that good in her mouth. She opened wider and took me into her throat, her nose nuzzling the tight curls at the base of my cock. My chest was heaving, and sweat was making my clothes stick to me. All I could think about was making her take it harder and faster; wanting to make her gag on it.

The pleasure and lust made me feel like a different person. Feeling a dominance I'd never experienced before. I released the counter and fisted my hands in her curls as I licked my lips when her eyes met mine. She slowly let my dick slip from her mouth.

"Not enjoying yourself, Daddy?" She asked the question already knowing my answer. She went lower to tongue and sucked my sac, rolling her tongue around them.

My grip on her tightened as I brought my right hand to curl around the base, and I pulled her back far enough that I could paint her lips with my precum.

"You know I'm yours, but this"—she kissed the head of my cock—"is all mine. Tell me what you want to do to me, Daddy."

I licked my lips, searched for the words to explain, but there weren't any. "I want to face fuck you until you have to swallow every drop." No matter what I thought, how I felt in control—how I craved dominance—I knew Sari was the one who ruled. She gifted me with that sense of power.

"You can do what you want to me. If I want you to stop, I'll tap your thigh twice, okay?"

I nodded. "Open wide, babygirl." Her eyelids grew heavy as she opened, and I thrust forward, releasing my dick so I could sink every inch into her hot, wet mouth. I held her head in my hands, forced her to remain still for me to fuck between her sexy lips. My stomach muscles tightened, and I grunted, using her to get off. My cock and balls ached so much when her throat gave as I bottomed out.

"So sexy. Fuck, you're so beautiful taking my cock. One day I'm going to fuck your tight ass." I froze with her swallowing around the head of my cock. She tapped my thigh twice, and I backed off, ready to pull out, but she sucked hard. "That's right, babygirl, work for Daddy's cum."

I didn't recognize my own voice, and my self-control was gone. I felt my release coming, and there was no stopping it. I met her gaze, saw the small quirk to the side of her mouth, and fire burned in my veins as I gave her all my thick inches and spilled down her throat. Cursing and shaking at the rhythm of her swallowing, I released her and collapsed back against the counter.

She stood and captured my lips. I parted them, and she shared my release with me. I sucked my flavor from her tongue. Her thick length pushed into the curve of my belly. I pushed my hands beneath the leggings at her hips and eased her pants down as far as I could.

"I'm going to suck that pretty cock. Can I do that, babygirl?" I saw her shock at my words, but she stepped back, so I fell to my knees just as she'd done. She was firm and heavy as I circled the base. The dark, flushed head teased my lips. Most of the women I'd dated in the past wouldn't let me give them oral.

I parted my lips and took just the tip in, learning her taste and texture. The flared head felt odd on my tongue, but I loved the hot, smooth length of my babygirl in my mouth.

"Just suck what you can, Daddy. Was I that sexy sucking yours?" She squeaked as I sucked her in deeper. I found the depth that triggered my gag reflex. "Damn, Daddy." I observed her face, took in her expressions, every hitch in her breathing or her sexy whines. She was longer than me, but more slender. I could only take half without gagging. She didn't seem to mind. Her one hand was in my hair, and the free one batted my hand away, squeezing the base, and she grew harder in my mouth.

"Play with my tits, Daddy."

I did as she asked as I suckled her pretty dick. She let out a steady stream of moans and gasps as I gave her head. Her little pebbled nipples grew into points, and she arched into my hands. My jaw ached as I sucked just the first two or three inches. I played with every inch of her. I lost track of time because it was only marked by the shallow thrusts of her hips—moans and whimpers, sharp pants as she cursed and called my name. Her dark skin was slick under my hands, and I slipped my fingers into the crease between her ass cheeks.

She tensed as I stroked over her clenching, wrinkled hole. I rubbed and fingered the hot skin but never entered her. She grabbed my hand and brought it to her mouth. And just like our first night together, she sucked my fingers, getting them nice and wet. Her gaze begged me for something, and I went back to torturing her tiny entrance and wondered how it would feel around my cock when she let me have her. Her thighs shook against my forearm, so I increased the pressure until just the tip of my middle finger entered her. At the feel of her tightness, my cock tried to harden again.

"Daddy, I'm gonna—" Her upper body curved over me, her upper belly on the top of my head as she jerked, a small amount of fluid spread over my tongue, and she let out a pitiful little whine as I swallowed. Suddenly she pulled from my mouth, and she fell to straddle my thighs.

We kissed for long minutes, each gentling the other as we brought ourselves back. Both of us a mess with our clothes eschew, and neither of us seemed to want to fix them.

"Thank you," she whispered as she hugged my neck.

"For what?"

"I was worried about, you know."

"It's your body. I find every inch of it sexy. I need a bit more practice, I think. Yet I'm sure with you that'll happen. But are we ever going to do this in a bed?"

She giggled. "Well, we christened the couch and now the kitchen. Lots of rooms in the house before we get to your bedroom."

"Will you stay in my bed tonight? I love sleeping with you in my arms."

"I kinda like it, too."

I worked her leggings back over her hips and tucked her tenderly back in. My shorts were working on cutting the blood supply to my thighs. I helped her stand and straighten, and she returned the favor of pulling up my pants. My dick was semi-hard and her tucking me in made me groan.

"One night, I gotta find out what your stamina is like because this"—she gave me a gentle squeeze—"is ready for another round. You liked giving your babygirl head, Daddy?"

"You know I did and playing with that tight ass of yours. I'm gonna split you so wide when you finally let me have it."

"Soon, I just..." She stopped talking.

"Babygirl, if this is all you're comfortable with, then I'm happy with it. Penetration isn't everything. There's plenty of ways to love on each other."

"I'm a little scared."

"Why?"

"I haven't bottomed in a long time. I take a lot of prep, and I've had a few lovers who didn't take the time I needed. Some got frustrated."

"I just gave you head for however long it took. I, um, did some research to know what to expect. How best to please you."

She hugged me and buried her face against my throat. She seemed to inhale deeply as if taking in my scent, and I did the same. I lived for these moments where I had her in my arms, held tightly against me. "Of course you did. You're considerate like that. Would you mind sleeping in my room so Reggie can find me?"

"Anything. Let's get ready for bed. It's getting late." I pulled away. I checked to make sure the kettle had turned off. I left her only long enough to grab us bottles of water and returned to her to lace our fingers. My compulsion to touch her, hold her hand was getting harder to deny as we pretended to be friends. I smiled as I led her upstairs, realizing that time was over. She was mine, and I couldn't wait for everyone to know.

19

SARI

I sat behind the table, signing copies and trying to keep the smile on my face. The reading I did before the signing still had my face heating. It's one of the things I hated the most. Reading my book aloud. I'd practiced with Drake, and all he wanted was the sexy parts, and that ended with heavy make-out sessions and mutual orgasms. That I wouldn't complain about.

Mental exhaustion had set in, and all I wanted to do was go home to my baby and Drake. Yet, I was there for a few more days. I had one more signing at a bookstore on the other side of the city. Since I'd adopted Reggie, I'd never been this far from him. I hated it, and Janice was trying to tell me to enjoy my time away.

That wasn't how I worked. I sneaked a sigh of relief when I saw there were only a few people left in line. I glanced down at the pen in my hand. It was a very expensive fountain pen Drake had gotten me for Christmas and said every author needed a fancy pen.

Finally, I placed my pen in my bag and stood up. I was hungry and getting cranky. I also wanted to check my phone to see what my family was up to without me. I slipped on my trench coat and slung my bag over my shoulder.

"They couldn't get enough of you." Janice was giddy as she stopped beside me.

"What did I say about my trips away from home?"

"It was only three days."

"Three days. I said no more than two, and I won't get home until the fourth day. I have a son. He takes precedence over all of this. I don't like being away from him and my boyfriend this long." My lips twitched at saying boyfriend. We hadn't sat down with Reggie yet, but we weren't hiding. We'd thought if we acted natural, he wouldn't see anything wrong with the shift in our relationship.

"I promise this is the only two-store stop. We need food." She slipped her arm through mine. After a quick stop to talk to the owner, we exited the store, stopping on the sidewalk. "When did you get yourself a boyfriend?" she asked.

After moving to a small town, I learned I loved the peace and quiet, the laidback life I'd settled into. Everything in the city was so loud and dirty, and it made me anxious. I pulled on my leather gloves and realized the temperature had dropped several degrees over the afternoon.

"Drake Pike. He's Reggie's principal. We started spending time with each other and became friends."

"Friends to lovers, very popular trope."

"You're not using my relationship as promo."

"I wouldn't do that. There's a restaurant at the end of the block. Let's just go there, and then we can get a car back to the hotel."

"Sounds good."

"Is it serious?" she asked as we strolled down the block.

"Yes. We've kinda taken things slow because of Reggie. He really likes Drake, and I don't want him hurt if it doesn't work out."

"Why is your first thought that it's not going to work out?"

"Maybe the fact that I'm a forty-year-old introverted single mom who hasn't had the greatest dating history."

"That's because you always hung out with that group of friends you had. There's nothing wrong with being a commitment-phobe professional or whatever, but you're very much the mom who wants one of those relationships."

"I know."

"So, tell me about this Drake."

"He just turned fifty. He was a teacher before he became principal. He's from a close family. What can't I say? He's sweet and gentlemanly, opening doors, making my plate before his, and making sure Reggie and I have everything we need before he even thinks about himself." I pulled my phone out of my bag, woke up my phone, and searched for the picture Drake had sent me earlier of him and Reggie. "There he is." I handed over my phone.

"Sexy and distinguished. How's the sex?" I jerked my phone away from her as she laughed.

"That's none of your business."

"That good, huh?"

I rolled my eyes at her grin, but I didn't say anything as we separated to enter the restaurant and saw the bar packed, but several tables were open. A hostess led us to a booth away from the chaos and took our drink order. I removed my coat and slid into the booth.

"Are you doing good, Sari? We don't spend as much time together as we did when you lived in the city."

"I'm doing good. It took a little bit to get used to the pace of small-town life. I mean, Clarkston isn't a tiny town, but it's a lot more laidback and quieter. Drake's family is amazing. They took Reggie right in. He has a better social life than I do."

"That's not surprising. You were never the life of the party. I wanted to talk to you about something, but the boyfriend might be an issue."

"I already told you, you're not my type."

"You're so not funny, Sari. That's one thing that hasn't improved."

"Drake thinks I'm hilarious."

"That's because he doesn't want to sleep on the couch."

"Drake doesn't factor in right now. What's going on?"

"You know I was dating that guy a few months ago?"

"Yeah, you thought there was potential there. What's wrong?"

"I'm pregnant."

"Um, honey, that's one thing you never wanted. Are you okay?"

"I don't know. I'm stressed. I'm not mentally or emotionally prepared for this."

Janice grew up in foster care, too. It's one of the things that had built our relationship, but they'd removed her from her home because of abuse. It was a long cycle of generational abuse; she'd been sixteen when she'd given up the baby from her first pregnancy.

"You know I'll help in any way."

"How would you feel about becoming a mother of two?"

"What?" My voice cracked. An odd feeling exploded in my chest as if the floor dropped out from under my feet.

"Listen, I'm a great aunt for the space of a few hours. I don't have the patience for a child. When I gave up the baby back then, I felt nothing when I looked at her. I carried her for nine months, every kick or movement, and I just don't think I'm the mother to bring up a child."

"You have options, Janice."

"I know, and I debated, but I can make a family happy. I thought I could make you happy. You're an amazing mother."

"How would—" I stopped talking as our drinks arrived, and I told the server we needed more time. She said she'd check back shortly. "How would you feel about seeing the child?"

"When I took the test a month ago, I felt nothing, not fear or happiness. I was completely indifferent. I'm thirty-eight...I have the life I want. I'm too selfish for a child. You know I'm obsessively careful, so the pregnancy was a shock. Figures I'd get pregnant with a condom and the pill."

"And you think I'd be the one to raise them?"

"Yes. In such a short time, you made Reggie safe and content. He has no doubts that you're going to be there for him. But the question is, does your new boyfriend possibly want to be a father of two?"

I sighed heavily. "I'll have to think about it. Not that I don't want to, but there's Reggie. I have to see if he wants to be a brother. There's also Drake. Let me get home, talk to him and Reggie. How much time do I have?"

"Seven months. Toward the end, I'll start arranging to put them up for adoption. I don't want you to stress about this. When I sat down to go over my options, I may be incapable of raising them, but there's someone out there who could give them the love and care I don't know if I have. So, my decision to place the baby for adoption is already set. It's just waiting to see if it'll be an open one with you or a closed one with someone else."

"Just give me a little time. You know if you need anything, you can call me."

"I know."

"What about the father?"

"Already asking when he can sign away his rights. He's older with grown children, so he has no interest in starting over. I already had the papers drawn up. We're meeting when I get back so he can sign. Him and I are not the parents for this child."

"Just give me a few weeks. I've never had a newborn before. Reggie was already past the middle of the night feedings and diapers stage."

"If you decide to do it, you'll be amazing. I know you will, Sari. You've been my best friend for a long time. I made it out of foster care, but the trauma of my birth family still haunts me. You made it out strong and ready to take on the world as the person you knew you were. You've always known you wanted to be a mother. I like not having to worry about anyone else. I can't even keep a relationship because I just don't form attachments. I'm always waiting for them to be like my family. You hate when I say it, but I just think I'm broken."

"You're not broken. You just know yourself and your limits. Even if I can't do it, you're going to make some person or couple whole. And there's nothing more awe-inspiring than that."

"I promised myself I wouldn't do this." She swept tears from under her eyes. "I'm always waiting to be judged."

"That's on them, not you. You know what's best. They don't live in your head or know what you've experienced. What did the doctor say?"

"Because I'm sickeningly health-conscious and obsessive about working out, I'm in perfect health. They said I would have to ease my workout routine the farther along I got. He put in my file that I was considering adoption and adoptive parents may be present for appointments."

"I really am...I don't even know what to say that you'd..."

"You're welcome. All I've heard for a decade was you wanted to be a mom, so you were the first one I thought of. Let's have dinner. We'll get through the signing tomorrow, and then you can go home to your little family. Take your time, Sari. There's no pressure."

I nodded as we both reached for our menus, and I barely saw the words. Another child, a baby, and I didn't admit, even to myself, that my first thought was to scream yes. I had to take Reggie's feelings into account. Would he want a sibling? Were we already adding Drake, so would a baby be too much change for him? I never even wanted him to contemplate that he was going to be replaced or that I'd love him less.

When I got home, we'd discuss it as a family. This would be a family meeting. But would Drake want to be included in a growing family? Who's to say he'd want to start taking care of an infant at fifty. Was I ready to do it at forty? I pushed it aside and spent time with Janice. I had missed spending time with my friend and agent. She was very much city while I was discovering small-town worked just fine for me.

20

DRAKE

I looked up as I felt myself being watched and found Reggie at the end of the couch. His arms were crossed, and his chin rested on them. I was reading to try to distract myself. Sari had been away three days, and I'd taken off half a day to go pick her up the following afternoon. She'd sounded exhausted when I'd talked to her earlier. I hated that I couldn't be there to take care of her.

"Couldn't sleep?"

He shook his head. "I miss Mama."

"I do, too, son. Come here." I patted the spot beside me, and he walked around the couch, climbing up next to me. He leaned his head against my arm. "You can stay up with me for a little while, but you have to go to bed. You have school in the morning."

"Mama will be home when I get off school?"

"Yes. I'm going to pick her up, and we'll be at school to pick you up." I lifted my arm and wrapped it around him, feeling him cuddle to me. "Do you have something you want to talk about?"

"Are you and Mama boyfriend and girlfriend?"

"If we are, what would you think about that?"

We hadn't exactly hidden our affection for each other. When

we were together, we'd cuddle up on the couch while Reggie would lie on the floor to watch TV or read a book. Other than the fact we hugged or touched, mine and Sari's relationship hadn't changed. We'd acted like a couple before we even shared our first kiss.

"You can't leave."

"Why would I leave?"

"Family isn't supposed to leave."

"I adore you and your mother more than anything. Leaving never crossed my mind."

We'd fallen into a routine since Thanksgiving. Weekends were at my house with the required ladies' nights and dinner at my parents'. Sari shared my bed, and Reggie had settled into the room I'd given him; he'd even started leaving things, or if I bought him something, he always asked if he could just leave it in his room.

Spring would be coming soon, and we'd been together for months. We were already planning a big summer vacation—a few weeks of just the three of us. Principals worked year-round, but I saved up my vacation. Unlike previous years, I wouldn't be staying home to work on my house.

One thing we hadn't discussed was a definite future yet. Over our time together, I'd fallen hard for Sari, and I wanted to tell her. But as much as I wanted to confess, I didn't know if she was ready. I wanted to know if she wanted to move in, build a life; I hated the saying I wasn't getting any younger, but it was true. My fiftieth birthday had passed. Although, being a public couple was still new for us.

"I know having your mama away is hard, but she has to work, and the occasional trip is part of that. Yet she will always come home to you."

"I just get scared when I can't see her."

"You can be scared. All you have to do is talk to me or your mama. You can always video-call her at any time. Do you want to see if she's awake?"

He nodded, and I stretched to get my phone off the coffee table. I quickly connected a video call and waited for her to answer. Her beautiful face filled the screen, and her lips stretched into a bright smile.

"My two favorite men. Couldn't sleep, love?" He shook his head. "I'm sorry. I'll be home by lunchtime tomorrow. I promise no more long trips. I don't like being away from you two. Drake said you went to grandma and grandpa's this morning."

I couldn't take my attention from her as she curled up in a bed too far away from me. She had on her bonnet to keep her hair from going frizzy. She'd given me a step-by-step how-to with her hair one night before bed. I loved the process and being able to sit on the counter in the bathroom and watch her. Everything in me wanted that every night—us putting Reggie to bed, and then me leading her upstairs. I loved the domesticity of all of it.

"I helped with the flower garden. Uncle David said he was going to make it pretty when spring started. He said I could help."

"Are you excited about that?"

"Yes, I get to help pick all the flowers. For here, too."

"For Drake's garden, too? You're going to be so busy. You going to have time for your boring non-gardening mother?"

"Always."

"I know, love. When I get home, I won't have to go away for another two weeks, but you're having fun staying with Drake, right?"

"Yes. We went to the shelter today. He was looking at dogs."

I saw her look at me and smile. We'd discussed if Reggie was ready for a pet, and I said he was and that I'd take him to look to see if any caught his attention. His process was pretty serious, and while he'd liked several, he didn't seem to find one he connected with.

"Did you have fun?"

"They let me play with them in the outdoor area. There were so many."

"Did you find one for Drake?"

"No. None of them were right. He needs just the right dog."

"I'm sure you'll help him find the perfect one. If you go to sleep, I'll be there even sooner. Can you try to sleep for me? You need your rest for school."

"Okay, Mama. I love you."

"I love you, too. I'll see you as soon as you get off school. I promise."

"I know, you never break a promise." I watched them as they talked for a few more minutes, and she blew him a kiss.

He eased off the couch, and I turned to see him climbing the steps. I didn't turn away until I saw him disappear into his room. When I turned back, I found her staring at me.

"You look tired, babygirl."

"I am. Too much going on. Way too many people to deal with. Is my boy okay?"

"He just misses you. I do too."

"I miss you. I told Janice that I wasn't happy about being away from you for four days. It's too long."

"It is, but you have to work, and this isn't a regular thing. You just have to get through another two weekends of peopling, and you can be back in your office."

"I can't wait. Drake, I appreciate you keeping him occupied."

"You act like it's a hardship. It's not. This is what a partner does for their person."

"And that's still new for me. When I get home, we have to talk."

"Talks aren't always a good thing, babygirl. Something I should be worried about?"

"No." She rolled her eyes and shifted in bed. The phone shifted outward, and I saw her bare shoulders. "What do you think about children?"

"You know I adore kids, kinda helps with my job."

"What would you think about dating a woman with two?"

"You going to adopt or foster another?"

She sighed as the phone moved as she rolled to her back. "Janice told me a few days ago that she's pregnant. She said she thought about asking me if I would be interested in adopting. I still have to talk to Reggie about being a big brother, but this decision also affects you."

"I only have one question you need to answer. Do you want to do it?"

"Yes. But this isn't bringing home another five-year-old. This is an infant. We've only been dating a handful of months…that's asking you to compromise a lot."

"No, it isn't. I love your son. I live for the two of you being around. So we'd have to work out how to add another to our little family we're building. I'm not going anywhere. You want to be a mother. I always wanted to be a dad, but that never happened for me. When I met you, I got just what I wanted. We'd be like any other couple having a baby."

"You're way too good at this shit, Drake."

"What? Do you want me to throw a man-baby fit? Maybe demand that you don't do it. That's not me, Sari. Also, you didn't see the way your eyes lit up when you said yes to my question. Yes, Reggie is going to need some time."

"Well, he has eight months to get used to it. I'll have to move my office to the living room or my bedroom. I'll need a nursery. It's not like I have to take leave from work when they're born."

"You've already been planning it."

"Maybe a little bit."

"I think more than a little, babygirl." I opened my mouth to ask her to move in since there was plenty of room for everyone there. She could take the library room for her office. There were two free guest rooms, but I felt that would be pushing it. I had months to get her used to the idea of making my house our home.

"I admit to nothing."

"When you get home, we'll talk about everything you and Janice discussed, and then come up with a good plan to talk to Reggie. All his cousins have siblings. He might like the idea."

"I was going back to fostering at some point after Reggie became more comfortable with sharing me. He's been good about sharing me with you."

"Babygirl, you're not alone anymore. You have me, and my family has adopted you. This isn't something you'll do have to do single. You know you have an exceptionally handsome and helpful man now."

"One who's modest as well."

I let out a loud laugh. "If this is something you want to do, we'll work it out so that you can."

"Thank you. Why do you make everything sound so easy?"

"I don't make it easy. I just know what makes you happy. Being a mother is one of those things, and you'll be ecstatic to be the mother of two. And down the road, you can foster again. Any child would be lucky to have you." I saw her eyes well up with tears. "Oh, babygirl, don't do that."

"I was worried." Her voice cracked. "I'm forty soon, and you're already fifty. A baby is a lot of work. I didn't know if you'd want to deal with all the stuff a new baby brings."

"Now, you don't have to worry about it. It's off your shoulders. Nothing changes with us. I still want to be with you and want this family of ours to work…and, in this case, grow."

"You're too good to me."

"There's never too good. I want you to go to bed and get rest. You're coming home tomorrow. I'll be there as soon as the plane lands. It's been too long since I got to hold you."

"Sleeping sucks without you."

"Then I'll bring you home, and you can curl up in bed with me."

"You know I do have a house."

"Yes, but you like it better here."

"You're sure of yourself."

"I am." We exchanged goodnights, and I reluctantly ended the video call and instantly missed her.

When I relaxed back into the cushions, I realized I hadn't stopped smiling. There's never been another person in my life who made me as happy as her. I could see a future, her in my bed, Reggie settling into his room, and a nursery. I might have thought about having kids, but I didn't look at it as a reality.

That was until a beautiful woman walked into my school with her adorable son and changed the entire course of my life. I wouldn't change it for anything. I wanted it all. We'd work everything out because as much as I gave up on finding some happy ending for me, I'd found it with Sari and Reggie.

21

SARI

I was in the basement of Drake's house doing laundry. My washer had started to skip the spin cycle. I'd discovered it when I'd gone home the previous day and started to wash the clothes in my suitcase. Drake's brother, Nolan, was coming to check it later in the week. Reggie was seated on top of the dryer reading as I separated clothes. I'd grabbed Drake's hamper since I was doing mine anyway. He was still at work, so as soon as I got the washer going, I was going to see what we had to cook for dinner.

"Will I have a brother or a sister?"

My son was obsessed with what his sibling would be. We'd had the talk as soon as I returned home from my work trip. He'd gotten quiet for several minutes, and I'd let him process. Then he asked when we were having them. I had to explain that his Aunt Janice would be having them for us and that it was still months away. I should've waited a while before I told him.

I snorted as he fired more questions at me. Worse, he'd caught me going over the list of doctor's appointments Janice had emailed me and made me put them on the calendar so that he could count down.

"What do you think we should make Drake for dinner?"

"I'll go look." He held out his arms, and I lifted him down, and he was on the move. I chuckled. I didn't remember my quiet son having that much energy before we moved there.

When I'd called Janice to say Reggie and I wanted to adopt the baby, she asked did my man feel the same way. I'd easily said yes. It wasn't only Reggie who was stalking the calendar, and the man was a manic mess as he'd made lists of the safest products. He told me he couldn't make every appointment, but he wanted to be at any when we could see the baby. I'd promised I'd let him know.

I'd even relayed all the stories to Janice, and she'd laughed. Then she demanded to meet him. There was one more signing in the city, so we'd planned a weekend away. Draven and Lanie would watch all the kids that weekend. All my friends were coming with their husbands. They'd have dinner and a night out, but I'd already booked a hotel room.

We needed to get all our alone time that we could get before the rush to get a nursery ready to bring a baby home. I also wanted to get my next novel done so I could take a few months of parental leave. I've never taken care of an infant before. I'd started to read up on everything and looked into childcare classes. Lanie and the ladies said they'd be there every step of the way, whatever I needed, advice or a shoulder to cry on.

I put the first load of laundry in the washer and turned it on with Drake's clothes mixed in. I only had three loads. I'd need to wash clothes more than once a week when my baby came home. A smile tugged at the corners of my mouth, and I couldn't believe I was going to be a mother of two.

My brain tried to misfire, assault me with fear. Every time my life seemed to be going too well, I always looked for the catch. I was on the way up in my writing career, I had an amazing son, and my relationship with Drake couldn't be better. No, I wouldn't anticipate the bad. I'd worked hard to make it to this point in my life. Other women like me didn't always have this chance to have a person and family. I wasn't going to take any of that for granted.

I jogged up the basement steps, and I heard Reggie's voice coming from the kitchen. The basement entrance was all the way at the back of the house. The Victorian had three rooms and a kitchen on the first floor, one large bedroom and two smaller ones, and a bathroom on the second, and the third was just a large open space with a bathroom that would elicit envy. I loved the house. Drake had shown me before pictures, and I couldn't imagine it as the same place.

I entered the kitchen to find Drake going through cabinets with Reggie.

"I didn't hear you come in," I said as I approached. He turned his head, and I brushed a kiss to his lips.

"Double-timed the never-ending paperwork so I could come home since I knew you two were here."

"I grabbed your laundry to throw in with ours."

"Babygirl, you didn't have to do that."

"I didn't mind. You have more dry cleaning than laundry. Do you want me to drop it off tomorrow?"

"Do you mind? They're never open when I go through town."

"No, I don't mind. We were going to make you dinner."

"Babygirl, you've been working all day, and now you're washing my dirty clothes. I'm going to see what we have, and then I'm going to change. Me and little man here are going to make you a feast, a feast I tell you!"

"What? Is he going to help you pick a takeout menu?"

He grabbed his chest and stumbled, pretending Reggie was holding him up. "Ouch, baby, that hurt."

My son shook his head and huffed. "Now I have two weird parents. Don't one of you have to be normal?" He stomped off, and I chuckled at his over-dramatic toss of his arms in the air.

"He said parents." Drake sounded strange, and I jerked my

gaze to him to find him staring at the entryway Reggie disappeared through.

"What's wrong? We knew it was going to happen." I closed the distance between us and twined my arms around his neck. He stared into my eyes, and the awe there was unmistakable. Reggie had accepted Drake as a part of our family, saw him as a dad, and I didn't want my son to ever lose that.

"Yeah, but…hearing it."

"Are you okay with that?" I was concerned it was too much to hear.

He frowned at my question and hugged my waist. "Of course. Why wouldn't I be? We're dating. You're here every weekend. We're preparing for a baby. That's as official as it gets. I want you to move in."

That feeling of the floor disappearing from under my feet happened for the second time. "Drake."

"I know. You're not ready, but that doesn't change the fact I want it. You can think about it, and when you're okay about the idea, you can tell me. We're doing this at a pretty fast pace, and the fourth member of our family arriving added another element. A lot of changes at once, but I need you to know, you and Reggie belong here with me when you think the time is right."

"I'm sorry, I just…" He dropped a kiss to my mouth. "I keep saying I'm all in. Yet here I am, still holding back. This is me. I'm always waiting for shit to go up in flames, you know? I don't want to be that way. You're going to get tired of my bullshit one of these days."

"Babygirl, look at me." I lifted my gaze to his. I hadn't realized I was staring at his chest. "If we don't work out, I love Reggie like he's my own, and that won't change. I'll still be Dad or the father figure…the other weird parent. I promised him family stays."

"You already talked about this?"

"Yes. He told me family doesn't leave, and I told him I adored both of you. You know I never make a promise I can't keep. He'll always be mine if you allow me to be there until he turns into a teenager, and he'll really be embarrassed by both of us. Never wanting to come home, spending all his time with his friends that we're not going to like."

"You're making being a parent of a teenager, oh so, appealing." I sucked my teeth at him.

"You're welcome." He grinned, and then he kissed the end of my nose. I wiggled it as his goatee tickled me.

"I'm going to be fifty-eight, almost fifty-nine, when this baby graduates."

"I'm going to be sixty-eight. What's your point? Are you having doubts about the baby or shackling yourself to a man on the edge of being decrepit?"

"Be quiet. You're not going to be decrepit. You're just going to get sexier. That's the way it works with men." He drew gentle circles at the base of my spine, and I snuggled closer to him. His warm, big body with his sexy belly was created just for me. My heart had claimed him as easily as it had when Reggie came to live with me. Yet the words I wanted to say wouldn't come. What amazed me was he'd give me all the time in the world. He wanted me to be sure before I made any decision.

"You'll be as beautiful then as you are today."

I felt my cheeks heat at his compliment. I should've grown used to them, but each one still took me by surprise. He always made everything right for me. He didn't tell me that my caution hurt him; he was too understanding for his own good. Although, complaining about his compassion didn't cross my mind for a second. Everything about him did it for me, and his sweetness made him irresistible. Some women might not see him as perfect as I did; that just meant he was all mine. Their loss was definitely my gain.

"What are you thinking about?"

"That the women who didn't want to keep you don't know what they lost."

"I think I remained single for you. I don't know if I believe in fate, but the moment I saw you...I was willing to do anything to have you."

His mouth came down on mine, and he kissed me—an action that was filled with everything he felt for me. All the love and devotion. We might not have said I love you, but it was there in everything we'd done. The acceptance without expectation. He gave me the choice, and I was in control of how fast or slow we went. He wanted me to move in but wouldn't give me an ultimatum.

"I want to move in, but I need to take care of preparing myself to be a mother of two. One day I will tell you I'm ready. Please don't get tired of waiting for me."

"I've waited a lifetime for you...a few more months is nothing as long as you're mine."

22

DRAKE

The bookstore was packed, and the line in front of Sari's table seemed to get longer. I watched her closely, and I saw she was quickly becoming overwhelmed, but a bright smile still curved her full, red lipstick-stained lips. Her success and strength caused pride to fill my chest. I always stayed within eye-sight of her. I'd quickly noticed that every few people she searched me out.

"They're eating her up."

I glanced down to find Janice standing beside me. When we'd arrived, she was in agent mode. Networking, and she rarely looked up from her phone.

"She's talented, and all her readers know it. I've noticed they keep filing in."

"Her time is almost up, and you can have her all to yourself."

"I'm going to pamper her when we get back to the hotel room. She deserves to enjoy a bit of quiet." I smiled at Sari as she glanced my way. "How are you feeling?"

"Good. My first pregnancy was terrible. I was sick the entire time, but I don't know if that was stress because I was a knocked-up teen or just how I react. I haven't had any morning sickness yet. Excited about the baby?"

"Very. Thank you for this. I won't pretend to know what it'll be like, but you're making my girl happy."

Sari had told me some of Janice's past with her permission. Yet not many details. I knew she'd grown up in a horrifically abusive home. Her first pregnancy was a result of an attack by her stepfather. When she'd started to show, the guidance counselor at her school had asked if she was pregnant. She'd confessed to what had happened—what her home life was like, and the authorities were called.

Social services had removed her from the home, along with two step-siblings. She'd lost track of what happened to them. The post-traumatic stress disorder rode her hard.

"Am I making you happy?" I heard the insecurity in her voice.

I didn't hesitate in my answer. "I can't wait to meet my child." Anticipation bloomed brighter every day, and I could imagine everything about my future. We were on our way to cohabitating. She and Reggie were at my place more than theirs, and she'd turned the library into her office. We still had nights apart. Disagreements happened, but nothing outside the usual couple fights. I wouldn't admit it to Sari, but I enjoyed our fights, too.

"I was a little wary of you." I frowned as I looked at her; she studied me as if I were a strange creature she hadn't seen before.

"Why?"

"You're too good to be true. You two aren't even living together yet, but you're all-in to be the partner…to be a dad. No one is that perfect."

I chuckled. "I'm nowhere near perfect. I'm a middle-aged, never been married, serial monogamist. I'm probably affectionate and gentlemanly to the point of annoyance. My parents have been married for half a century with five kids and twelve grandkids, including Reggie, and they still act like newlyweds. I've always wanted that, but the pressure to find what some would call a fairy tale is immense. My siblings found it and made me jealous as hell."

"That must be nice."

"Sari said the same. I won't say I understand what you and her, or even Reggie, have gone through because I can't fathom taking something I've always dreamed of for granted. Their experiences brought them to me, and I won't regret or take that lightly."

"Still too damn weirdly perfect."

I chuckled as I caught her impish grin. "As long as my woman thinks I'm perfect, I'll deal with being weird."

"I'm glad she found you. She needed nice. She started to give up on the partner front the last several years. I better get back to work. It won't be too long, and she's all yours."

"I'm here whenever she's ready." I meant that in more ways than one.

As much as I wanted to rush forward, I had endless patience when it came to Sari. She wanted me. I wanted her. We'd made plans, just not in terms of timeframes, but everything was set in motion. There wasn't any drama or miscommunication. We discussed everything—any worries we had, decisions were made like any other family. We just had our own version of what that meant.

I crossed my arms over my chest and focused on my woman. She was beautiful in her body-hugging red sweater dress and her favorite pair of black stiletto boots, and she'd been so nervous about the night that she'd put her curls in a cotton turban. Watching her, I could see how proud and confident she was in her career but wasn't comfortable with all the praise. She'd told me creatives were their own worst critics. Other than her practicing her readings with me, I hadn't taken the time to read anything yet. I'd gone through and bought all of them in e-book and paperback. She'd rolled her pretty brown eyes at me when she'd noticed them on a shelf all by themselves.

"I would've given you copies, Drake."

"I know, babygirl. But I wanted to support you." I wanted to soothe her as I noticed her discomfort. "I haven't read them yet."

She moaned and tipped her head back, showing off the elegant line of her throat. I wanted to press a kiss to the curve. "Don't let me know you read them."

"Why not?"

"I don't know." She pouted and threw a mini-tantrum.

I smiled at the memory and the smirk on her face as I backed her up to the heavy wooden desk and made her forget about being embarrassed. We hadn't broken apart until we'd heard Reggie groan at his disgusting parents kissing. She'd shaken her head at my stupid grin. He still called me Drake, but one day I hoped to be Dad.

As I'd lost myself in my thoughts, the line had shortened to only a handful of people left, and they'd placed a sign to say it had ended. While she'd taken an afternoon nap, I'd gone out and got her favorite lotions and bath oils, several battery-operated candles, and a bottle of Champagne to celebrate the end of the first of many successful signings in the future. Before we'd left the hotel room, I'd placed the bottle in the mini-fridge in our room so it would be chilled when we returned.

I had the entire night planned. I'd draw her a bath, and while she enjoyed some quiet, I'd order room service. Then I'd prepare her for bed. She deserved anything I could do to make her happy.

When the last person thanked her and walked away, I approached the table as she pushed up from her chair. I slipped my arm around her waist, rested my big hand on her hip, and leaned in to press my lips to her cheek.

"I'm so proud of you, babygirl."

"Thanks. Do you mind if we skip dinner? I just want to go back to the room."

"It's all planned, bath, room service, and the two of us just enjoying some time together."

She sighed and turned to hug me. "Sounds perfect. I'm so glad this is over."

"I know you are. Anything else left to do?"

"No. A thank you to the owner and manager. What's in the bag you put with my purse?"

"Books for Reggie about being a new brother. Also, some books on what nervous dads need to know."

She quickly pressed her lips to mine and pulled back because our kisses usually got out of hand fast. I was still unsure of this new dominance and strong sex drive I'd developed. She reveled in our sexual relationship, and I did too, but I also loved the hours we spent touching and kissing. Both so on edge that we couldn't wait another second. I removed her jacket from the back of her chair and held it out, causing a sweet smile for me as she turned and allowed me to help her on with it. And then I picked up the shopping bag.

"Let's go. We can call Reggie and tell him goodnight, and then the rest of the evening is ours."

"Perfect." We walked to the counter, saying the requisite goodbyes and thank-yous to the manager.

I led her outside and stopped her to button up her coat and make sure she was nice and warm. She reached for my hand and twined our fingers together. We were only three blocks from our hotel.

"Did the girls have fun?"

"They had a blast. I know they wanted to stick around, but I told them to go enjoy their kid-free night."

"They deserve it. It's so rare for them to have a night away."

She rested her head on my shoulder as we walked, and I turned to kiss her forehead. "Did I tell you how beautiful you looked today?"

"Um, I think you may have mentioned it once or twice. You're really slacking today."

A rumble built in my chest as I released her hand and put my arm around her waist. I wanted her closer. No one else existed on the sidewalk as we made our way to our room. I noticed a couple of stares as we went. I was sure we were an imposing sight at our heights and sizes, but I didn't care. I'd be glad to get home where I didn't have to share her with anyone other than Reggie.

When we finally reached our hotel, the doorman opened the door, and we both thanked him as I let her go first. I placed my hand on her lower back as I led her to the elevator, stroking my thumb on the indent of her spine. I couldn't wait to get my woman alone.

23

SARI

The hot bath was heaven. I'd carried a tenseness all day that I hadn't realized. My friends from the city had arrived before the signing to ask if I wanted to go out and party with them. I'd had to decline. They'd tried to talk me into it until Drake stepped up beside me. I couldn't keep the smile off my face as I'd introduced them. We'd made superficial plans for another time.

At the thought of Drake, I turned to find all my favorite bath and body products lined up on the edge of the tub. Through the open door, I heard him ordering our dinner. I'd told him countless times he was going to spoil me. I thought I should've felt more overwhelmed by the attention but realized that I'd learned to relish all that he was.

"Dinner will be up in thirty. How are you?" He spoke as he entered and then crouched down beside the tub. He stroked his fingers over my forehead and straightened my shower cap, tucking a stray curl under it. I rubbed his bare chest with the back of my hand, and the hair teased my skin. I shivered, thinking about what those crisp curls felt like on my smooth skin.

"I'm good. Fuck, I needed this."

"I figured you did. About halfway through, I saw you struggling."

"How did you notice?"

"Babygirl, you know I can anticipate all your moods."

"You're such a good Daddy to your babygirl."

"That's all about you." He leaned in, and as soon as his mouth touched mine, I forgot all my stress and exhaustion.

We both chuckled as I wrapped my arms around his neck and pulled him forward, water splashing as he braced his left hand beside my hip on the bottom of the tub. I gasped as he cupped and rolled my sac in his calloused hand. My thighs parted as wide as the tub allowed as he played with my hole.

Except for the tease of a single finger, sometimes his tongue, he never touched me there. We hadn't done penetration, but we'd learned a lot of ways to get off without it. I had to admit I wanted it. I knew he'd never rush me; if I said I wasn't ready, he wouldn't push.

"I want you to fuck me," I whispered against his mouth.

"Are you sure?" He pulled back enough to see my eyes.

I nodded. "I like being fucked but..." I didn't know how to explain it.

"In the past, they didn't make sure you were ready. That'll never happen with me. You know I'm happy without it."

"I know you are. I trust you, but the last few men soured me to bottoming. The longer I'm on the hormones, the longer it takes to get off. You've never seemed to mind."

"Babygirl, hours of touching you, hearing those sexy gasps of yours when I touch you just right, what the hell would I have to complain about? Don't even get me started on giving you head until you're pulling my hair and squeezing my head between those soft thighs." He punctuated each word with a touch, and the drag of his short nails up the back of my thigh drew goosebumps out on my skin.

"I brought supplies…just in case."

"Then you finish your bath, we'll have dinner, and then do whatever feels right. Is that okay?"

I leaned up to push my mouth to his and sucked at his firm bottom lip. He groaned as I trapped it between my teeth. I slowly released the curve. "That will work for me."

He pinched my chin and gave me a quick kiss, and then he straightened to leave me to take my bath. When I was left alone, I stroked my soft length where it rested on my lower belly. I'd gone the week before and had my usual wax, so I was nice and smooth.

I let the water out and stood up to turn on the shower. I'd planned to suggest we have penetrative sex, so I'd prepared myself before he'd arrived to pick me up. It had been so long since I'd prepped for sex that I'd felt a bit awkward. I used my loofa to scrub every inch of me.

Once I finished, I stepped out of the shower, removed my shower cap, fluffing my curls, and picked up the tub of cocoa butter. Wrapped into a towel, I walked out into the main room. I froze in my steps as I saw the room. Candles lit the room, food waited out on the table, and a bottle of champagne was placed in an ice bucket. A red nightie I hadn't packed spread along the foot of the bed.

"No champagne glasses, but I didn't think you'd mind. I forgot to ask room service to bring some."

"What did you do?"

"I said you needed to be pampered. Let me have that." He held out his hand, and I gave him the lotion. He removed my towel with a tug, and it fell to the carpet. He sat on the edge of the bed and arranged me between his spread thighs. "Just trust me, babygirl. I just want to make you feel good."

My nod was permission enough, and he massaged the cocoa butter into every inch of me, front and back. I shivered and arched into the sensual press of his hands. He massaged me to relax me, but I was anything but. When my back was to him, he curved his slick hands around the front of my thighs. I threw my head back as he kissed down the indent of my spine, and I sighed as he pressed his lips to the top of my crease. I grabbed his hands in a tight grip as he nuzzled between my ass cheeks.

"Time to get you fed, babygirl."

"Tease."

"Only for now. You need food in your belly. You were too nervous to eat a proper lunch." He stood, and I spun to face him. He had lotion on his face, and I rubbed it in as he smiled at me. He circled my nipples with his thumbs.

"Keep that up, and there won't be any dinner." He smirked down at me and then excused himself to wash his hands.

All I could do was just stand there and take it all in, everything he'd done for me in the short time we'd known each other. He made everything so right without even trying. I jumped as I felt his fingers drawing my hair from my neck, pressing his face into the curve. He sucked but not hard enough for a mark. He always saved those for places only we could see.

"As much as I hate it, let's get you dressed."

He slipped the nightie over my arms and head, smoothed it over the thickness of my body, and led me to the table to eat. I'd never grow tired of this.

WITH FULL BELLIES, he had music playing on his phone, and I reclined between his legs on the bed. Since we were both naked, the hairs on his chest, stomach, and thighs teased me. He drew slow circles on my belly. We'd already told our boy goodnight before I'd gotten in the bath. All we had to do for the rest of the evening was focus on us. I had plans for my big man.

I leaned forward and batted his hands away when he tried to keep me close. Once I was on all-fours on the edge of the bed, I glanced over my shoulder to find him focused on my ass. I hid my smirk as I crawled the rest of the way off the mattress and walked to my bag. I quickly found the condoms and lube.

I straightened and turned back to the bed to find the bed turned down and him leaning against the pillows. The way he looked at me, the heat and lust in his gaze, made me conscious of every curve of my body. It was a good awareness because I knew he loved my shape. Instead of my usual trepidation of allowing someone into my body, I longed to feel full. To know it was him loving on me.

"Two taps to my thigh, and it ends."

I smiled at what had become our signal. Sometimes our lovemaking became too intense. His stamina was off the charts, and I felt a bit smug because I knew that was all because of me. I placed the items on the bed and joined him, straddling his thick thighs. His cock was already hard against my soft one.

He slipped his hand beneath my curls and curved around the back of my neck. My body melted into his so easily, and his lips touched mine. He loved on my mouth tenderly, and I gripped his thick hair in my hands. Our tongues touched and danced; our breathing increased. His free arm hugged my waist. A shiver worked through me as the coarse hair on his chest teased my sensitive breasts. My hips became restless.

I chased his mouth as he retreated. "No, babygirl. I want you to turn around and show me your sexy ass." He pinched my chin. "But remember, at any time, we can stop."

My heart was beating so fast that I could barely breathe as I turned and straddled his thighs. I whined as his hands stroked over the curves of my bottom, along my spine, pressing the center of my back. He urged my upper body down until my face was buried in the comforter between his calves. I tried to suppress the tremors that were part apprehension but mostly excitement.

He gripped the fleshy curves of my ass cheeks, spread them wide, and the warmth of his breath and swipe of his tongue over my hole had me throwing my head back. He groaned as he ate my ass, pushing at my tight rim, and I sunk my teeth in my lower lip to keep from screaming. I reached back to grab one of his hands to ground myself as the pleasure turned to torture.

How long had it been since I trusted someone enough to open myself? I rode his face, rutting against his tongue as I felt the pressure of the tip slipping inside. I lost track of time as he painfully gripped my hips and jerked me back while he fucked me with his tongue. I clawed at the comforter. Begged and pleaded, I didn't care how I sounded or how desperate I acted.

"No," I whined as he released me, and I scrambled to turn around, then he roughly pulled my mouth to his.

Every inch of my body was on fire. I trembled and set my softness to jiggling. My mouth fell open as cool, lube-covered fingertips massaged my hole.

"I'm gonna eat that pretty ass every fucking chance I get." He growled as the tip of his middle finger pushed inside. He rubbed around just inside. He'd played with my ass before but never penetrated me with more than a fingertip because I wasn't ready.

At that moment, I was more than ready, and I was impatient. "Now, Daddy."

"No, babygirl, not until I get you nice and ready." His tone broached no argument, and I squealed as his right arm gripped my waist to flip me onto my back.

I fisted my hands in his chest hair as he added more slick and pushed in a second finger. He scissored as he licked and sucked over every inch of skin he could reach, nipping sharply at my nipples. His skin was covered with sweat, easing the stroke of my hands over his back until I barely felt the brush of his breath before he swallowed my cock. It was too much, the thrust of his fingers and the suction as he gave me head. I hugged him to my groin as I squeezed his head with my thighs.

My shoulders lifted from the bed as a scream locked in my throat, and then he was gone—my release kept from me. I opened my eyes to find him on his knees, and his hands shook as he tried to get the condom on. I cupped my balls, my nails teasing over my stretched hole. He wiped his hands on the t-shirt he'd discarded earlier on the side of the bed.

"Fuck, I'm never going to get enough of you just like this." I almost started to tease until he laid down on top of me. His weight was heavenly as it bore me into the mattress. I held my breath as I felt the thick head press to my hole. "Babygirl, if it hurts at any time, we're going to stop. Do you understand?"

"Yes. You'd never hurt me, Drake." Even as I said it, I braced for the pain as he slid in so slowly that all I could do was sigh. He cursed as he rested his forearms on either side of my head and kissed me with such tenderness tears welled up.

"This feels so..." He clenched his jaw when he was finally seated fully. "Right. I'm going to love you so good, babygirl."

This wasn't fucking or just sex. Out of all the times we'd loved on each other, this was making love. He kissed me between smooth thrusts and retreats. The pressure and burn were unlike anything I'd ever felt before. His skin, his body, the wetness of sweat, I gripped his sides and scored his back with my nails. My every moan was nothing more than a sigh of breath as he told me how beautiful I was. How I was born to be his.

He used his steely control as he aimed for my gland, rolling his hips and grinding against me, teasing my hardening cock. He knew what I needed. He never grew frustrated when I needed more. I clenched down around him, and he rumbled deep as his lazy pace quickened. His strokes were deeper and harder until his hips met my ass—the slap of sweaty skin grew louder.

He held me close, enfolding me in safety as he began to fuck me. His body arching and slamming into mine as I begged for more—harder. I felt so outside myself. I couldn't breathe or think; all I could do was feel as the heat built. My ass taking everything he wanted to give me. I writhed beneath him, and then he pushed up without pausing and wrapped his hand around my cock.

I watched him through a blurry haze as I fought to draw in enough oxygen. Then my lungs seized, and I bore down on his cock, coming so hard nothing existed but his loving gaze locked on my face. I wrapped my legs tighter around him, dug my nails into his skin, and I whined long and low as I found my release.

"Babygirl!" he shouted as he thrust so hard it pushed my hips higher off the bed. His head thrown back, his neck muscles stood out starkly. I swore I could feel him pulsing as he filled the condom, and I hated that I couldn't feel his seed inside me.

We were both breathing fast and ragged, and he barely caught himself when he collapsed on top of me. His mouth found mine for lazy kisses as we kept grinding together, drawing out our releases until we weakly cuddled in the middle of the big bed.

"Are you okay, babygirl?"

"I'm perfect, Daddy. Drake..." My voice broke, and I noticed the tears slipping down my temples. "You were perfect."

"Sari, thank you for trusting me."

I whimpered, and he hissed as he slipped free. He rolled to his back, taking me with him. I curled against his side.

"I'll get us cleaned up in a minute. You wore your old man out."

"But you're my old man." I brushed a kiss to his chest as I hugged his chest with my left arm and never wanted to move.

"Damn right I am." His fingertips danced over my hip as our bodies calmed and cooled until he was forced to get up to dispose of the condom and get a rag to clean us both up.

How the hell had I ever lived without him?

24

DRAKE

Spring was in full swing, and the work on my gardens started, which took up most of my weekends. Reggie remained by my side—he loved being busy and helpful. Every Thursday, Sari and I attended a childcare class. Her nerves got the best of her about taking care of an infant because she'd never been around one. I'd babysat my nieces and nephews, and I'd promised to help. Told her new parents never really knew everything.

At the beginning of the school year, the best I could say was that I was content with my life. Seven months later, I had Sari and Reggie. A woman I loved more than anything and a little boy that I considered my own. We still went at Sari's pace, but it hadn't skipped my attention that they spent more nights at my house than hers. She mainly went there to work, then she'd return to my home with Reggie for dinner, and after we tucked him in at night, she was all mine.

Everyone I worked with commented that I'd changed; that I seemed happier. Most of them knew I was dating Sari since we'd made our relationship public. I didn't hesitate to walk Reggie out to Sari when she'd pick him up. My arm would automatically wrap around her, and she'd offer her cheek.

I couldn't remember being happier than I was at that moment. We were on our way. Slow and steady didn't bother me. I wanted her sure about us; I didn't want to have any doubts about how we felt about each other.

There was a knock on my door, and I told the person to come in.

"Mr. Pike, Reggie Hampton had an accident at recess. The nurse said he's going to need stitches, but he didn't lose consciousness."

I was already out of my seat as soon as she'd said he'd had an accident. Sari had added me as his emergency contact and the only other person allowed to take him from the school. I hadn't bothered with a suit jacket, and all I had to do was grab my keys.

"I'll be taking him to the emergency room. If you need me, you can reach me on my cell. Call his mother for me, please." I rushed past her and down to the nurse's office next to the gym. As soon as I entered the room, I grimaced, seeing him with a bloody towel held to his forehead. My chest tightened with fear, but I hid it to make him feel okay.

"Son, what happened?" I crouched in front of him and removed the towel to get a peek. Definitely needed stitches, and head wounds always appeared worse due to bleeding.

"My hands slipped, and I fell." He had tears dotting his lashes, and his voice broke a bit.

"Come on. We're going to head to the ER. They're calling your mama now. She'll probably be there before we will." I picked up his backpack they must have gotten from his classroom, and I took his hand as I stood, then we headed for the door.

"The nurse said I need stitches. Is it gonna hurt?"

"I won't lie, they're going to numb it, but it's gonna sting first. After that, it'll just feel like someone's tugging as they stitch you up. But me and your mama are gonna be there the entire time, I promise."

"I'm scared."

"And I told you, it's always okay to be scared. I was scared when they told me you were hurt, and I couldn't get to you fast enough."

After we crossed the employee parking lot, I put him in his booster, which he was saying he was too big for. His doctor told us differently. That didn't mean he hadn't argued his case to me and Sari, and then to both of us over dinner. The trip to the local hospital didn't take long, and the best thing about a small town was that the ER was never too busy.

"My son fell at school. He's going to need stitches. Has his mother showed up yet? Sari—" I didn't have time to say her last name before I heard the doors open behind me and her calling Reggie's name. She wore my t-shirt and sweats, probably the first thing she grabbed. She tended to be a lot more undressed when she worked.

"Oh, love, let Mama see." She was on her knees, checking him over. She hissed as she removed the towel.

I wanted to comfort her because she was on the verge of tears. "He probably just needs a few stitches, babygirl. He's going to be fine." I suppressed my grin at her very mama-bear glare as she nearly threw his insurance cards at me. "I did play football. I've had a few myself. It looks worse than it is, I promise. Would I lie to you?"

"No, but he's all bloody. What happened?"

"I was crossing the monkey bars, and my hand slipped, and I couldn't catch myself. I hit one of the bars."

I gave the person at the desk his insurance cards, and almost immediately, we were taken back. Sari sat with Reggie on one of the hospital beds with an arm around him while the nurse examined him and her free hand held mine. Like with any trip to the emergency room that wasn't critical, we waited for a doctor. The longer it took, the more irritated my woman became, but I lowered to sit beside her.

I tried to comfort them both until the doctor entered the

room. He double-checked Reggie's pupils, then removed the bandage the school nurse had put on him.

"The gash is deep, so he's going to need it stitched. Okay, Reggie, this is what we're going to do. We're going to get a needle with some medicine. It's going to hurt a little, more like a sting."

"Dad already told me."

My chest tightened, and for a minute, all the breath left my lungs at hearing him call me Dad for the first time. I rubbed his back and hid my smile at his annoyed tone. He hated when people talked down to him. The doctor gave him a comforting smile and told him to lie down. Sari took one side, and I took the other as he squeezed our hands in his tiny ones.

We only moved enough for the nurse and doctor to work.

"Love, just keep looking at me, and when we're done, we'll go home."

"Dad's house."

I glanced at her to find that bright smile on her face that I loved. The one that showed off her cute dimples. "Yes, Dad's house. That's where I worked today."

Reggie's every flinch made a tear slip from the corners of Sari's eyes, so I alternated between drying her tears and his. He relaxed when the medicine kicked in, and they quickly closed the two-inch wound just below his hairline.

"I'm sleepy."

"When we're on our way home, we'll go through the drive-thru for some dinner, you can have that, and we'll curl up to watch a movie."

"You're still crying, Mama."

"I know, but Mamas get to do that when their babies are hurt. I don't care if you're six or twenty-six. It's not going to change. Get used to it, love."

I chuckled at his long-suffering sigh, earning a smile from him and a glare from my babygirl. After they finished, they gave us a list of things to look for—I'd had a few concussions in my life, so I knew all the signs. Sari signed all the discharge papers, and I picked him up. He laid his head on my shoulder.

We hadn't been there long, but it was already around dinnertime. "I'll follow you two home. It's too late to go back to school." I checked my phone and didn't see any texts or messages from work, but word had apparently made it back to my family. Probably one of the kids told my siblings.

I followed her to where she'd parked in the lot across the street and got Reggie in his seat, buckling him in. Once I had the door closed, Sari wrapped herself around me.

"Babygirl, it's okay." I rubbed her back as I felt her grip the back of my shirt.

"Thank you for being there."

I pressed my lips to her forehead and inhaled the sweet scent of her hair. "You're welcome."

"Is he going to be okay?"

"He'll be perfect. We'll give him some children's pain reliever and get him some dinner. Do we have any at your house? I can stop and get it."

"We still have the bottle from when he had that cold at Christmas. I put it in the medicine cabinet in Reggie's bathroom."

"Do you need me to stop and get anything from your place?"

"No, I did laundry, so we have clothes."

"Even if you didn't, you look good in mine."

She let out a giggle and relaxed against my chest. "I was folding them when the school called, but I have to admit they're pretty damn comfortable."

"Let's get our boy home." I gave her a slow, tender kiss, and I stroked her soft cheeks with my thumbs to wipe away the last of her tears.

I waited until she was in the car and pulling off toward home. As her SUV disappeared, I slipped my phone back out of my pocket and called my mom.

"Do you not know how to check messages?" my mother practically yelled at me.

"We just got out of the ER."

"How's my grandson?"

"He's fine. He didn't lose consciousness when he hit his head, but he opened up a nice gash. They stitched it, gave us signs to look for. We'll have to go to his pediatrician to get them removed."

"Do you need me to watch him tomorrow?"

"They said he should be fine, and I don't think Sari is going to let him out of her sight."

"Understandable, but let her know if she needs grandma to come sit with him while she works to call me."

"I will. Mom."

"What's wrong?"

"He called me Dad."

"Felt good, huh?"

Good didn't even cover it because I'd waited months to hear him call me that even though I knew he considered me one of his parents. "Yeah, I'm still in the hospital parking lot. I better get going."

"Just remember, if you two need me, let me know."

I thanked her and told her I loved her and then disconnected the call. I walked to where I'd parked on the other side of the lot. Sari would worry herself sick if I wasn't there to distract her. They needed me, and I didn't want to be anywhere else.

SARI

Our nighttime routine became my favorite part of the evening after putting our son to bed. I sat crossed-legged on the sink counter in our private bathroom. Drake was just a fuzzy outline through the steamed-up glass shower walls. My notebook was forgotten where I'd rested it on my thigh. His big body was perfection to me in every way. He was just perfect. When I'd met him eight months prior, I hadn't seen myself here.

"I should use you as inspiration for all my stories," I said as he turned off the water and pushed open the glass doors. "I do have some scenes I may need a bit of help with. You know logistics, hand placement... all that stuff."

His gaze stroked over my nakedness; the need I saw aimed my way was addictive. "If I must."

I flipped him off as he chuckled, his laughter briefly muffled as he dried his hair, and I set my notebook and pen aside. When he crossed the large space, I uncrossed my legs, and he stepped between my bare thighs. Water beaded in his thick body hair, and I moaned as he gripped my hips to tug me to the edge of the counter. I draped my arms over his shoulders.

"I love you." He looked shocked for a split second before he took my mouth in a brutal kiss. His hard embrace forced the air from my lungs.

"I love you so much." He breathed roughly, his hairy chest rubbing against my breasts. My small nipples beaded.

He kept kissing me, only stopping long enough to gaze at me with such happiness on his face. No one had ever looked at me like that—made me feel like he had in our months together. I worried I'd say the words too soon. That a part of me would want to withdraw them to protect myself, but he said it, too. His voice was so full of reverence and passion.

"I'm ready to move in. I figured we needed to get the I love yous out of the way if we're going to cohabitate and have a baby together."

He picked me up, and my legs instantly wrapped around his waist.

"I'm taking it from your reaction that's good news?"

"The best. What made you change your mind?"

"Nothing. I think I've been ready for a while. The few nights a week I force myself to go home, I'm miserable. I love being able to have family dinner…tucking our son into bed, and then having you and me time. Curling up in bed with you. Knowing that when you touch me, you can't imagine doing anything else. I worried I wouldn't be enough. And before you say anything, that didn't have anything to do with something you did."

I held on tight as he carried me to the bed and laid me down, then he quickly stretched out beside me. I slipped into my favorite spot in the house, curled against his side, playing with the thick hair on his chest and stomach.

"You'll always be enough. You gave me everything I've always wanted. A woman to love. A family of my own. You don't know how much it killed me to give up on that dream, and the joy I felt when I met you nearly took my legs out from under me. What else could I want other than you and our son, our baby on the way? I know it seems quick, but..." He paused as if he searched for the right words.

"It's just right. I definitely didn't see myself here when I brought Reggie to school."

"That's because you thought I was an asshole, but you were wrong because I was charming." He chuckled as I growled at him and lifted to straddle his hips. I shivered as his cock notched between my ass cheeks.

"You were an asshole, and you know you were, but I still love you anyway. Even though you're getting old and forget things." I laughed as he gasped and looked at me in horror.

"That's just...I don't even have a comeback for that. You say you love me and then call me old. I'm so not feeling the love right now." His fingertips stroked up and down my thighs.

"Oh, be quiet. You know I don't want to be anywhere else. Besides, old or not, you're sexy."

"You're just on it tonight. You're in an ego-destroying mood."

"Good thing you think I'm sexy." I arched as he drew the backs of his fingers up my belly and around my breasts, quickly pinching my nipples. A whimper slipped free. "I love when you touch me."

"I always want to touch you. You make me lose control so easily. I love that you fit me so perfectly."

I laced our fingers and brought them to my mouth, brushing kisses to his knuckles as I took in the way he looked at me. There was heat, but there was also love because he accepted everything about me. Made me believe in the happily ever afters that I'd only written about. It was all fiction until I'd met him.

"Hey, what are you thinking about?"

"I didn't believe I'd find anyone that made me feel as if I fit. There was a time where I didn't think any of my dreams would come true."

"You deserve everything, babygirl."

"I know. But when you grow up as a Trans woman, especially

a Black Trans woman, you're not shown many positive examples of everything you can attain. Stories about Trans people are often tragic. You'll be ostracized. More often than not, the news is violence against us."

"I won't say I understand what it was like to grow up, to find your place, but I'm sorry it was hard for you."

"I know. You have a loving and accepting family. But it wasn't just coming out. It was also the insecurity that foster care gave me. It took forever for me to believe that not everything or everyone was...temporary. Sometimes I still have a hard time accepting that I have a son I adore, a sweet, sexy man, and a career that gives me financial security. I'm forty, but part of me is still that kid who never thought any of those silly fantasies would come true."

When he sat up and brought his lips to mine, I closed my eyes at the first brush. As much as I loved our sex life, the kisses, cuddles, and all the random touches eased the anxiety I still fought against. Some nights that's all we'd done. I loved the easy intimacy of our alone time.

"You're perfect. The first time I spotted you, I thought you were adorable."

As I groaned, I made myself heavy—adorable was the kiss of death. He chuckled as he gave me a shake.

"Stop that. That cute snarled nose of yours got my attention."

"You have weird triggers, Daddy."

"No I don't because really everything about you does it for me."

I rolled my lips between my teeth, and my goofy grin probably made me look silly. Yet he always knew what to say to make me feel good.

"Is that so?"

"Yep, you know I ain't made it a secret you're just my size." He palmed my ass cheeks that overflowed his big hands, and I shivered. "You feel so good and make me feel so right."

"That's because you are," I whispered against his lips. "I'm a selfish bitch because I'm glad no one got you before I did."

"Possessive, that's kinda sexy."

"Only kinda?"

When he tipped his head back as if thinking, I tweaked his chest hair and glared at him. "You gotta stop doing that. With those tugs when you're annoyed with me and the handfuls you get when I'm fucking you, it's a wonder I don't have bald spots."

"You like when I hold on when I ride you."

He groaned. "I really, really do."

"Then quit complaining."

"We're moving you in this weekend. I'm not giving you a chance to second guess. My woman and son need to come home all the time. Because this place is empty without my family in it."

I squeezed my eyes as a tear slipped free. When I tried to turn my face away to hide it, he pinched my chin.

"Don't do that, baby. I waited so long for you, and I don't want to spend another night apart unless it's work-related. I love you, and you brought me the best gifts, you, our son, and a baby on the way. It's time for our lives to start. We both have so much time to make up for."

If I wanted to speak, I'd found it impossible as he took my lips with his, and he kissed me until he rolled me beneath him. I'd never get tired of him loving on me.

26

DRAKE

I'd worked a bit later than normal as we were finally going to see our baby. They'd scheduled Janice for an ultrasound that next day which happened to be the Friday before Father's Day. I wouldn't be back at work until after lunch. Reggie had hung out with me. He liked staying after and helping the teachers clean up or organize for the next day. They all adored him and let him be helpful.

"Who are you?" Reggie asked.

I jerked my head up from the stack of mail in my hand to find Ellen standing outside our front door. I hadn't seen her in a year and a half. After we'd broken up, she'd moved to California for a new job. I didn't remember her looking so stiff and austere. Her long silver hair pulled into a severe bun.

"Son, here." Reggie took the key I handed him, and he unlocked the door. "Hang up your bag and take your folder in the kitchen and remember to knock to make sure your mama isn't busy working. We'll do your worksheets before dinner."

"I know, Dad."

I grinned as he disappeared inside, but he left the door open. His sneakers pounded on the hardwood floors. Sari would hear him coming from a mile away. "So much for him not disturbing his mother. What are you doing here, Ellen?"

"I just moved back to town."

"I have a phone."

"Had to replace mine and lost all the numbers. I knew you'd already left work."

"Come on inside. I have to see what to start for dinner. Sari's on a deadline, so she barely leaves her office until I make her." I motioned for her to go first. I might not like her just showing up out of the blue, but we hadn't parted on bad terms. I closed the door. "Go on back to the kitchen."

I observed her taking in the mixture of my laidback, classic style and Sari's bright fabrics and rich textures. I loved the eclectic mix of us everywhere in the house. Ellen wasn't a fan, and I could tell. She came to an abrupt stop at the family photos staggered on the foyer walls.

"Who's that?" She pointed at Sari.

"That's Sari. You want some coffee?" I passed her as I heard the TV come on in the family room. "Reggie, one game." I heard him yell *yes, sir*, and I continued to the kitchen.

"Last time I talked to Lanie a year ago, she said you were still single."

"A lot happens in a year."

"You did an amazing job with the house. Decorator went a little crazy."

I laughed to myself as I started the kettle, and then I spooned coffee grounds into the French press. My terrible coffeemaker was retired when my babygirl moved in.

"Sari did a perfect job," I said as I gathered sugar and creamer, placed them on the table. I pulled down three mugs. "Did you think—" I was cut off as Sari walked in wearing her shorts that barely reached her mid-thighs and a tight camisole. My babygirl knew what her work clothes did to me.

"I didn't know we had a guest." She continued across the kitchen to give me a kiss.

"Ellen, meet Sari." I introduced them as Sari turned to lean into my side.

"You're the ex. He told me you'd moved away for a job. Pleasure to meet you. Are you staying for dinner?"

"No. I just moved back to town, and I knew Drake had already left work. I stopped by on the off chance he was here."

"Well, if you change your mind, we always make plenty. Baby, Janice's appointment was moved up an hour, so we'll have to leave at eight instead of nine."

"One of us needs to write a note for Reggie missing school. He's still going, right?"

"Yes. We promised him that he could go for the first one to see the baby."

"I'll write one for his file when I get to the school tomorrow afternoon."

"Sounds great. I have one more chapter to finish, and then I'm all yours. You good without me?"

I grinned as she glanced at Ellen. "I'm good, babygirl. Remember you wanted to finish the book ahead of schedule for maternity leave. Now, get it done."

"Yes, sir. Sorry to run, but I'll see you at dinner if you decide to stay. Again, it was nice meeting you."

I didn't take my gaze off my woman until she exited the kitchen. She turned for a split second and gave me a wink. I was a little irritated that I didn't get my usual welcome home behind the closed doors of her office.

"Been dating long?"

"We met eight months ago when she brought Reggie to school the first day."

"Didn't think you dated student's mothers."

"Sometimes rules are meant to be broken. What are you really doing here, Ellen? A second chance now that you're back in town? I thought we made it clear we weren't right for each other."

"Time and minds change."

"They do, but not that much." I turned away and poured the water into the French press, stirred the water and grounds, and placed the push-down strainer on top. "You didn't want the life I wanted. I doubt that's changed all that much."

"Even if it had, no chance of that now. There wasn't anything wrong with the life you wanted. I was recently divorced and not ready for the second phase happily ever after."

"And that was fine. We ended things before anything got serious." I turned back to her, and she stared at me like I'd offended her. There was one thing that her and I never did, and that was argue. I didn't care enough to fight her lack of want for me. It was just what it was.

"We dated for two years. That's usually serious."

"Not enough, though, Ellen. You didn't want to live with me. We were just glorified friends with benefits, and there wasn't anything wrong with that. Sari wants all the things, we dated, we exchanged the I love yous, and we're having a baby in August. That's what I always wanted. Your plans and mine didn't mesh."

"We could've made it work." Her once beautiful face was pinched, her lips pursed, and I didn't understand what she was so upset about.

We'd dated two years without her mentioning any type of commitment. Had she expected me to still be single or that I would jump back into a relationship with someone who didn't value the same things? Not wanting kids wasn't an issue. She raised hers and didn't plan to have more, adopted or otherwise. But she refused to consider living together. A possibility of marriage. I'd wanted a full partner, and she hadn't reached the level of ready either of us needed.

"No. There was never a chance it was going to be long-term.

And I'm happy about that. We were complacent. We were a habit, and when we split up, it gave me the best opportunity."

"You didn't think about us at all?" I heard her voice harden.

I refused to lie. I questioned what didn't work, but I didn't think about her specifically. "No. When it was over, it was over. We'd both made it clear our dreams didn't line up."

"And *her* dreams line up?"

"In every way. She's perfect. She invited me into her family. Gave me a son I adore. We're adopting a baby."

"Aren't you a little old to be changing diapers?" I laughed at her snide question.

"No, I'm looking forward to every second of it. Every dirty diaper. Every sleepless night. I can't wait. Now, do you want to stay for dinner since Sari extended the invite?"

"No. I think we're done here."

"I'll walk…"

"No. I can find my own way out."

"Goodbye, Ellen. It was nice seeing you. We'll probably run into each other. I'm sure Mom and the girls would like to hear from you."

She didn't comment, and as she walked out of the kitchen, I didn't bother listening for the door to close. I turned and prepared coffee, put Sari's in a travel mug, and doctored it just the way she liked. Mine I kept black. As I was cleaning up, arms circled my waist.

"She trying to take my man?"

"Yes, she was." I smirked at her adorable growl and patted her hands. "Were you worried?"

"No, I'm not the jealous type, and I trust you to handle things yourself. Although, I did have a moment where I was about to throw down my hidden pettiness. She doesn't look like your type, Daddy."

"When she left, she didn't carry herself like that. She was always professional when it came to work. But outside that, she was fun, had a great laugh. I don't recognize her. She looks harder...a lot older. Maybe the new job didn't sit well with her, or her life hadn't been what she wanted." Once I washed everything, I spun in the circle of her arms and lifted my left hand to brush the spiral curls of her bangs to the side. When I stroked my fingertips down her rounded cheek, she leaned into my touch. "No one has ever acted as if they craved my touch before you. They didn't do this."

"This?"

"Touch me for no reason other than to feel me...to enjoy my presence. Touch meant they wanted sex, lights out, missionary as if the sooner it was over, the better."

"Daddy, what kinda people have you dated? At least your taste has significantly improved."

"There's my modest and sweet babygirl." I closed the short distance between our mouths to kiss her soft smile.

"You excited about seeing our baby tomorrow? Still no doubts?"

"I can't wait to see the newest member of our family, and I have no doubts at all. I never have. The minute I saw you walk into class that morning, I knew you had to be mine."

"Um, excuse me, Mr. Pike, but you were a bit of an asshole."

Our on-going disagreement about our first meeting made her gorgeous eyes brighten. "I remember the exchange quite differently, Ms. Hampton. I was exceptionally charming, and I don't know why you can't remember that."

A little snort escaped. "We'll have to agree to disagree. Go change out of your suit, Daddy. I'll start dinner. We have a big day tomorrow."

"Do you want to find out what the gender is?" I asked because I'd looked it up, and it was typically something they asked. I'd read every book I could get my hands on since I found out we were having a baby. Living with me or not, her kids were mine, and I'd made sure she knew that; that I wasn't going anywhere.

"No. But if you want to know, I'm okay with that."

"Doesn't matter to me. They'll be perfect no matter what."

"You might have to bring Janice a present. They told her they consider her pregnancy a geriatric one."

"Shit, do we have to find a new doctor?"

"It was close, so, so close."

"I love you, babygirl."

"I know, Daddy, I love you, too. Go get comfortable. I missed you today."

I cupped her cheek and nipped at her upper lip and then her lower one, sucking at the plush curves. She tightened her arms around me as she lifted onto her toes to press flush to my chest. When her lips parted, I slipped my tongue inside to meet hers. I groaned as I kissed her, and I reminded myself we needed to behave. Even as we tried to separate, we kept pressing our mouths together. Kiss after kiss until she pressed her forehead to mine, and we tried to catch our breath.

"Just be good until bedtime, and I'm all yours."

"You're all mine anyway, babygirl." I brushed my lips to her little smile and forced myself away to get a shower and change my clothes.

I didn't care how long we were together; I knew I'd never get enough of her. Her presence. Her smile. That special way she made me feel—as if I was the only man she'd ever want. I hoped that was true because I wanted to spend the rest of my life with her. One day I'd ask her—I'd been carrying the ring around for weeks. I'd be ready whenever she was.

27

SARI

My palms were slick with sweat, and I kept rubbing them on my skirt. Janice was already on the table, and the lights were low. She'd patted the spot next to her legs for Reggie to sit beside her. She wanted him to have a front-row seat to see his sibling. I felt like a bitch about my secret worry over what Janice would feel after she saw the baby. She kept reassuring me she didn't feel any more connection to this pregnancy than she had the first one.

Drake, Reggie, and I were so excited about bringing the baby home. Fingers laced with mine, and I glanced at Drake—he was watching me with a calmness I wasn't close to feeling. All those daydreams I'd had while I laid in a different bed almost every month came true, but I was terrified I'd wake up back in one of the foster or group homes to the painful reality that none of it was true.

I listened to the tech and stared at the screen with tears in my eyes as she pointed out fingers and toes, a perfect nose, and a beautiful tiny face. I squeezed Drake's hand as I leaned in closer, resting my cheek on Janice's arm.

"What do you think? Am I doing good?"

"They're perfect, th-thank you."

"You never have to thank me, Sari. You're an amazing mother. You and Drake are the only ones to raise them."

"Did you want to know the gender of the baby?" the tech asked, and I looked at Drake as she made some notes on the screen.

We'd talked about it, and we didn't want to know, but maybe that had changed seeing our child on the screen. Gender didn't matter to me...all I wanted was a happy child. I wanted to be able to hold them in my arms and discover what their personality was. Would they take after Reggie in temperament?

He shook his head and smiled at me. "No, we don't. Their assigned gender doesn't matter to us." He cupped my opposite cheek and pulled me to him to brush a kiss to my temple.

We watched as Reggie rubbed Janice's belly, talked to his sibling, and his eyes got so big when he saw them move on the screen. He was going to be an amazing big brother. The tech kept making notes and taking screenshots of our child.

She used a towel to clean off the gel on Janice's belly, and then she handed us a series of pictures.

"Janice, I'll leave you to get dressed. I know you're meeting with Doctor Birks, so we'll call you back for that shortly. Congratulations, Mr. and Mrs. Pike."

"Oh!" The hand that rested on my thigh drew my attention, and I turned to find Drake smiling, that soft, loving look in his green eyes. He always made me feel like no one else existed. I faintly heard the click of the door.

"Sari, I keep waiting for the right time, but with our children and your best friend in the room—" He reached into his pocket, and I held my breath as I saw him hold out a black velvet bag. "I don't know what I did so right to give me you and Reggie, but I'm not going to question it. I want to spend the rest of my life with you, raise our kids, maybe a few fosters, or adopt more. I want to be yours and Reggie's home as much as you're mine. Will you marry me?"

I glanced from his eyes to the ring repeatedly as I tried to figure out if I was hallucinating.

"No, baby, you're not hallucinating. What do you say?"

"If you don't say yes, I'm going to!" Janice yelled at me.

"Yes."

"Free will or Janice peer pressure."

"Free will." I gripped his face in my hands and leaned in to kiss his full lips roughly. "I want to be your home...we do." I glanced at Reggie. "What do you say about your old, embarrassing parents getting married?"

I laughed as Drake barely caught him when he launched himself at us.

"I take that as a yes. No complaints about me marrying your mom?"

"Nope. Now, you really can't leave."

"Reggie, I have no intention of ever leaving you. I promised, family doesn't leave, and I have no plans to break that promise any time soon."

I sat back to watch Drake and our son have a moment. They'd gotten close in so short a time, but I'd seen the unconditional love between them for months. Drake would always be Dad, and he'd taken the role without reservation. I still remembered the expression on his face the first time Reggie said it. I'd never doubted his feelings for us.

"You did good, Sari. I'm a jealous bitch right now." I jerked my attention to Janice, fearing what I'd see on her face, only to find her grinning at me. "I get to plan the bachelorette party, strippers, so many strippers."

We snorted at the warning rumble of my big man. Drake's warm, rough hand took my left, and I watched as he slowly slid the gorgeous ring onto my finger. It was just right, like everything about Drake and I. Maybe I'd fought it and had fallen into the what-if game. Yet he made everything okay with each kiss and act of patience as he waited for me to figure it all out.

He tugged me forward until I was close enough to brush his mouth to mine. "Love you, babygirl."

"Love you, too."

Janice let out a long sigh. "Damn, you two are so cute."

I flipped her off as I kissed my man and Reggie slipped from between us, muttering to himself about weird, gross parents. Drake's lips pulled into a smile.

"We're going out to celebrate. Reggie can miss one day of school."

"I'd like that."

"Thank you for saying yes."

"What else was I going to say? Would I say no to home?"

A knock on the door broke the moment, and I looked down at the simple diamond ring, spinning it around my finger as all the small lingering doubts disappeared. I'd spent more than half my life worried about finding my home—the family I'd secretly longed for. And I'd found it with my son, my man, and my best friend who was going to gift us with another child to love.

All of it came together as it was meant to be. I'd written all those happily ever afters for the couples in my head, and it was time I had my own. We led Reggie from the room to allow Janice to finish cleaning off her belly, and then she joined us as we planned for the future. It was perfect, and I'd never take it for granted.

EPILOGUE

DRAKE

Tears still unabashedly wetted my cheeks as I stared at my wife in the hospital bed. Our perfect daughter was cradled in her arms, and her focus was fully on Alanie as she checked her over. We'd both been in the delivery room with Janice. Our friend had been all smiles when she saw Sari with the newest member of our family.

I'd never expected the rush of love for someone only minutes old. When the nurse handed her over calling me Dad, it had all hit me. Our family of three became four. Reggie was on the way with my parents and the rest of my family to meet our daughter. We'd kept her name secret, a surprise for Mom.

"How was Janice?" Sari asked as she looked up.

"Sore and craving sushi. Davina's stopping to get her some and sneaking it in." Janice had started spending more time in Clarkston, and lived with us the final month of her pregnancy. She'd even liked the obstetrician in town better than the one in the city. My family had adopted her as easily as they had Sari and Reggie. Just like with Sari and Reggie, my affectionate and close family had overwhelmed her.

"How is she really?"

"I think she's good. She said she was happy to have her body back and that her niece was exceptionally beautiful, and we could thank her for that." I chuckled as Sari snorted.

I'd been worried about our friend. She'd carried our daughter for nine months, but even with Sari telling me to go check on her, I didn't see her lying that she was okay. She apologized that she didn't feel like a mother. She didn't feel anything but a fondness, and I reassured her that if that changed, she had to let us know. If she needed us to keep a distance for a while, neither of us would judge her for that. She'd given us the perfect gift, and that couldn't have been easy no matter the smile she tried to keep on her face.

"She really is perfect." We hadn't wanted to know what we were having because it hadn't mattered to us. Her nursery was an explosion of color, bright and as beautiful as my wife. She patted the mattress, and I didn't hesitate to take the spot, giving her a kiss and then brushing a gentle one to our daughter's forehead. She had these adorable blonde curls tight to her scalp.

She smelled of baby powder and a bit of Sari's lotion. I inhaled the scent of both of them into my lungs.

"How can you love someone so much at first sight?" she whispered in awe.

"Babygirl, it hit you twice. Reggie and now her."

"When can we take her home?"

"Tomorrow. We just have to spend the night." Reggie would fight us on it because he'd tried to talk us into letting him be in the delivery room. He'd given us the silent treatment every time he wasn't allowed to go to an appointment. As with everything, our son was serious and all-in. Sari swore he got that from me.

"Is everyone on the way?"

"Yes. Davina and Tolliver will be a little later because they have the special side trip to make. I'm not telling Janice she can't have her sushi. That might be dangerous."

A knock on the door preceded a nurse coming in. "Hi, I'm

going to be your night nurse. My name is Marcy. Are you two doing okay?"

"Yes, thank you," I answered as the nurse peeked at our daughter and then went to change the nurse's name on the duty whiteboard on the wall.

"We're going to try her first bottle in a while. Until then, you should have everything you need beneath the bassinet. Don't hesitate to hit the call button if you need anything."

As soon as the nurse left, the horde descended and surrounded the bed. Reggie hugged my dad's leg as he nervously locked eyes on his new sister.

"Hey, love, don't be nervous, come meet your sister." Sari held out her hand, and he slowly approached.

I lifted him onto the bed and sat down behind him as he leaned over to peer at Alanie. "She's so tiny." The awe in his voice was almost as deep as Sari's over our daughter.

"She is. We'll have to be gentle with her. But soon, she'll be up and running and annoying you just like a little sister should." Sari stroked our son's cheek.

"What's her name?" Reggie barely touched her forehead with his fingertips.

Sari smiled at me, and I took her as I carried her to my mother. "Well, everyone, meet Alanie Raven Pike." My mother's hands shook as she took her newest granddaughter. She pulled me down and kissed my cheek, and I started to back up, but my father grabbed the back of my neck. He leaned in and brushed a kiss to my forehead.

"You did real good, son." He released me to greet Alanie.

I went to the bed and lowered to sit in the space Sari made for me. I wrapped my wife and son in my arms. I'd spent so many years imagining this, but I kept it to myself because I'd thought it would never happen for me. All it took was the right person walking into my school and breaking my rule. It had brought me a wife and two beautiful children. I'd waited a lifetime for them; I'd never take that for granted.

"I love you, Drake," Sari whispered, and I looked away from the sight of our family passing around Alanie, but she kept making it right back into my mother's arms.

"I love you, too, babygirl." I crossed my right arm over my chest to cup her cheek, tugging her close and meeting her lips halfway. Her hand curved around my wrist. As I kissed her, everything else disappeared as I silently thanked her for the gift that was her and our children.

ABOUT THE AUTHOR

Siobhan Smile is an author of happily ever afters with a twist. They features characters of all sizes, shapes, sexualities, gender identities, and races. Reading a Siobhan Smile book lets you escape for a few hours whether that is to an alien world or a contemporary setting, you'll find something outside the norm. Writing books for Siobhan is more than simply telling a story, it's a way for everyone to see themselves get a HEA.

Author Pronouns: Nonbinary/Gender Nonconforming - They/Them

ALSO BY SIOBHAN SMILE

Little Love
His to Own, Hers to Claim
Shug's Daddy
Butcher's Babygirl